ANGELS
OUT OF THE DARK

By

J.S. Peck

BEJEWELED PUBLISHING
LAS VEGAS, NEVADA

Bejeweled Publishing
6480 Annie Oakley Drive
Suite 513
Las Vegas, Nevada 89120

ISBN# 978-0-9824607-6-4
First Edition: October 2020

COVER ART DESIGN: Kelly A. Martin
INTERNAL DESIGN: Jake Naylor

DEDICATION

This book is dedicated to the non-profit agency, Awareness is Prevention (AIP), and all the non-profit agencies and individuals who are working to clear human sex trafficking in the United States and the world. We aim to provide girls and boys a higher chance of having a childhood free from exploitation and the overwhelming sense that they are never safe. It is only when we say "Enough is enough" and work together that we have the power to eliminate what has become another kind of sickness that is so prevalent today and to create a better, safer world for all.

TABLE OF CONTENTS

CHAPTER 1

It was my turn next. I waited just beyond the curtains, and when I felt a tap on my shoulder, I made my entrance. With head held high and my footsteps weaving their special stage walk, I headed down the runway. I felt all eyes on me as I marched along, and I heard a few gasps of pleasure. The dress I wore was stunning, but it was my looks that had caused the stir. I could pretend it was different, but what was the point?

I halted and turned around slowly enough that the dress flowed with grace and allowed the potential buyers to get a better view of its loveliness. Then I strutted back to where I'd emerged. My tall stature, flowing red hair, emerald green eyes, and my slim body served me well as a model. The only thing that didn't quite fit was my large breasts, natural though they were. Sometimes, I needed to wrap them so I could slide into a particular style of dress to show the creation off to a better advantage.

Soon, I and some of the other models would head to Las Vegas for a photoshoot and a stay at one of the fancy casinos and resorts there. I'd never been to Las Vegas; I had only heard about it. It had grown quite a bit from its earlier days, and I wanted to see for myself what the fuss was all about.

"Tiffany, hurry!" said another model, pulling me away from my thoughts. "They want us on the runway again. They're going to introduce us to the audience sitting there."

"That's different, isn't it?" I asked.

The model bobbed her head and turned away to take her place in line. I followed. As I marched once again down the runway, I cringed upon hearing my name spoken out loud, "Tiffany Darling." It sounded so false, so fake. But, in fact, thanks to my parents, that was the name on my birth certificate. As young and as unworldly as they were, I felt sure that my parents had no idea the trouble that my name had already caused me so far.

Having come from a small city in Idaho at the age of 18, I was ready for a change and the big time. As I packed my bags for Las Vegas, my heart thudded with anticipation. My roommate and I collided at the doorway of the apartment we shared, and we laughed at our urgency to leave. We headed downstairs to meet the cab waiting at the curb to whisk us away to the airport.

After I settled into my seat and buckled up, we lifted into the air. The noise from the plane was soothing enough that I was soon slumped in my seat, asleep. Only later, when I felt the airline attendant standing over me, did I begin to stir. "Please put your seat upright. We'll be landing soon."

April was already straightening the items on the empty middle seat. She tucked the magazines into the back pocket of the seat in front of her and turned to me. "This should be interesting, huh?"

I nodded and gasped as I looked out the window. "Look outside! Where are we? There's nothing but mountains of rock."

April placed her hand on my arm. "It's okay, I promise you. Wait, and you'll see what I mean," she encouraged as the plane soon began its landing in the center of the city.

That time seemed so long ago. So much had happened since Tiffany had bounced through McCarran airport with stars in her eyes, happy to experience all that Las Vegas offered. She had no idea then what lay ahead for her, and if she had known, she probably would've never departed the plane. What came about was an extremely rough time in her life—a harsh time by anyone's standards. She had gotten trapped in the city's tar pit of destruction, where it was hard for anyone to escape. The irony was that, frequently, she needed to remember every ugly detail of what'd happened to keep herself on the straight and narrow. The Tiffany who had arrived that day from New York City so many months earlier was now nothing but a memory.

Instead, when she faced the past, it wasn't the glory days of modeling in New York City, it was the shame of what happened afterward in Las Vegas that twisted her heart:

She'd stumbled her way into the bedroom, nearly spilling her drink along the way. Filled with more vodka than ice, it was merely for comfort, not taste. How had things come to this?

She tripped, and the glass sprang from her hand, dousing the wall and carpet with the clear liquid that spread toward her bare feet. When the cold hit her toes, she jerked back. A more lucid reality of what'd happened came to her. She needed to get a grip, but how was she going to do that? Especially when the voice in her head became louder, making her cringe with the honesty of its words. "You're such a loser." And those words would be the kindest; always, her inner taunting became uglier in time.

She dropped onto the unmade bed and pulled her legs tight to her chin, aching for the darkness to take her away. Suddenly, the door flung open, and he stood there scowling. "You disgust me. Get the hell out of my house!"

She stayed still and pretended to be out cold, but he stepped nearer and stood over her. His foul breath floated around her, and it took all her control not to gag. "I mean it, bitch!" He yanked at her unkempt hair and pulled her face from the pillow. Tears leaked out and ran down her cheeks, giving her away. "I'd drag your sorry ass out now, but I'm late as it is. Gone by morning, hear me?"

She lay still. Where would she go? She had begun her downward spiral a few years back and had shut out anyone good in her life. Instead, she had fallen for the biggest loser of all time—snow—cocaine. And to feed its demand? Those were the times she didn't dare think about. They were nightmares all by themselves.

She felt blood trickle from between her legs, and the ache in her heart became unbearable. She knew she'd done the right thing, hadn't she? Wanting numbness, she reached for her drink and saw the glass on the floor, empty. Disappointment filled her as she realized she didn't have the strength to do anything about it.

Then, she forced herself up. Clutching herself, and bent so far over it looked as if she were crawling, she stumbled into the bathroom. There, she grabbed a washcloth and began her clean up. Finished with the bare necessities, she lurched her way back to the bed and crashed upon it, not caring whether she ever woke up or not.

Now eight years later, it was the memory of that night that pushed me each day to do whatever it took not to repeat that time in any way. It still took hard work at times for me to cut off that negative voice in my head and block any opportunity for it to begin its blasphemous chants. I'd been close to becoming a statistic wasted by drugs; yet, I'd been one of the lucky ones. By the grace of God, I had lived.

My cell phone chirped, and I was glad to see it was one of my two Samaritans who had saved me. I smiled. "What's up, Lester?"

As I listened to him, my frown deepened. "Where is she?" I asked.

I listened to Lester's calm voice "We'll meet you in an hour, okay?"

"Are you coming here?" I asked.

"Yes, we're on our way."

I looked around the office where I sat. The sign on my desk read, Tiffany Darling, Counselor, but that didn't cover it all. My thoughts turned to Lester, remembering the first time I'd met him.

She had crawled out of bed after that horrible night and jammed a few of her things into a cheap plastic bag advertising Marshall's, and stumbled out into the daylight feeling sick. She fingered her hair to give it shape and a semblance of style before she headed into the older part of Las Vegas. She'd be safe there before she went on the hunt to earn some money. Since she was still bleeding and not feeling well, she'd offer a blow job. Perhaps she'd be lucky and make enough money to feed herself for a couple of days.

Later, when she saw him get out of his car, she knew there was something different about him. When he reached her, he didn't pull her into the alley where she stood at its end or didn't immediately start fondling her or himself. Instead, he'd asked politely, "What's your name?"

"Tiffany. Why, does it matter?"

He leaned closer and, in a soft voice, asked, "Why are you doing this? Selling yourself like this?"

"Look, mister, I don't have time for your crap. Do ya want a blow job or not? Fifty bucks and I'll make you think the bells in heaven are ringing." She stood defiant in her stance until her legs gave way.

Instinctively, he reached for her and grabbed her arm, supporting her. Then, he held on tighter as he felt how hot she was. "You're sick. You shouldn't be here doing this stuff."

She straightened and yanked herself away from him. "What makes you think you have the right to judge me? Well, you don't, pervert. Mind your own business or I'll… I'll…"

He held his hands up in a defensive mode. "I can help you, miss. You're burning up, and you're bleeding."

Her face reddened, horrified that she hadn't noticed. A hot flash and then a wave of cold crossed her body. She began to shake, her teeth chattered, and she felt herself falling. His quick hands caught her, and he half-lifted, half-carried her into his car parked along the street.

My cell phone chirped, breaking into my thoughts. I read the text message. *Change in plans. Meet us at the house.*

I immediately rose, gathered my purse, and headed out the door.

CHAPTER 2

Thirty minutes later, I pulled into one of the many look-alike houses lining the streets in North Las Vegas, and the door opened as soon as I reached it. I smiled at the woman who greeted me. It was one of my Samaritans and best friend, Lucinda, who smiled back with white teeth glowing in coffee-colored skin.

"Who have we got here this time, Lucy?" I whispered.

"C'mon in and see for yourself," she answered, opening the door wider, lightly pulling me inside.

I stepped into the small living room where Lester was sitting on the couch with a tiny, Asian girl beside him. She looked like a frail little bird who'd fallen from its nest and wore two black eyes as if to confirm her fall. She couldn't have been more than 90 pounds and was skinny as a rail with fake boobs that made her look ridiculous and unappealing. Most men needed more than boobs to turn them on—that fact, most young girls today didn't understand until it was too late, and the damage to their breasts had already happened.

Lester held his arm loosely around her shoulders, comforting her as she cried. The odd thing was that many of the girls we'd helped through the years often rejected the women who wanted to comfort them, preferring a man instead. Johns and pimps gained such a powerful hold on their victims that many times it was the male power the girls trusted—usually gained through their abuse.

Lester rose from the couch and stepped forward. "Tiff, I'd like you to meet Sue-Ling."

I looked down at Sue-Ling, who hesitated to lift her eyes to meet mine. Instead, she furtively looked around her as if to seek escape, sending off a warning signal to me. As I made my way forward, my large size loomed over the tiny girl before I lowered myself and sat beside her. Sue-Ling shrank back and leaned away. I reached for Sue-Ling's hand and gently pulled it from her side, enveloping it in mine. In a soft voice, I said, "It's nice to meet you, and I'm glad you're here. You've made the right decision."

Sue-Ling sat quietly and still. In the same soft voice, I continued. "You're safe with us, and we'll help you change your life around. That's why you've come to us, isn't it?"

Sue-Ling nodded without looking at me.

"May I ask how you found us?" I asked, curious.

"One of the girls said to go to the soup kitchen on Martin Luther King Drive and ask them for help," she choked out, holding back more tears.

"Now that you're here, there's no turning back. You understand that we can't have you jeopardize the others involved, don't you?"

Sue-Ling nodded and then looked fixedly at me. "I promise."

"Lester wouldn't have brought you here if he didn't think you were serious about wanting out of the snake pit you're gotten yourself into. Okay, then. Let's get started. Grab your things, and we'll head out."

I felt a twinge of regret about this girl and looked to Lester. He lifted his brows in question. The feeling passed, and I quickly shook my head to show that it was nothing. Lester hadn't let us down yet. I thought it all must be in my head. I looked at the young girl and could only imagine how she must be feeling, like I, myself, had felt those many years ago.

> She had woken up in the hospital that day long ago to see Lester's worried dark eyes blending in with his skin. She started to get up from where she lay only to have him gently push her back down. "Just relax and let them do what they need to do so you can get better. Don't worry. I'll be right here."
>
> Too weak to do much else, she'd trusted him and his words. Then no longer able to fight sleep, she'd clutched his hand, closed her eyes, and whispered, "Please don't go." She never questioned why she'd ask that of a man whom she had just met—a man more than twice her

age and not anyone she'd be interested in on a romantic level. She hoped with all her heart that he'd be there when she woke.

Tiffany lifted Sue's bag and walked to where Lester stood. "Are you and Lucy joining us later?"

He kissed my forehead in a fatherly way. "Yes, we wouldn't miss it for the world."

Lucy came into the room. She hugged Sue-Ling and whispered something in her ear. Whatever she said made Sue-Ling smile, and again I became overwhelmed with my love for both Lucy and her husband. How had I been so lucky to have them come into my life?

Tiffany had woken up later in her hospital bed to find Lester had kept his promise and had stayed with her. Sitting there was a woman who looked not much older than she was, reaching for her hand. "Who are you?" Tiffany asked.

"Lester is my husband, and we're here to help you. My name is Lucy."

"I don't understand. Why are you being so nice to me?"

"If it were in reverse, wouldn't you do the same?"

Tiffany was quiet as she thought about what Lucy had asked. Would she? Honestly, she wasn't sure. She gave Lucy a vague nod and answered, "Maybe."

Lucy and her husband looked at each other and smiled. "Ah, honesty. That's an excellent sign, isn't it, Lester?"

"Indeed. It's a good beginning."

"What is it with you two?" Tiffany asked. "Want do you want?"

"Do you have a place to go to once they release you

from the hospital?" asked Lester, searching her eyes. The unspoken response was clear. "Would you like to hear what we have to offer?"

"You're not a john, are you?" she asked, tearing her hand away from Lucy's grasp.

Lester laughed heartily, and Lucy joined in. "No, Tiffany, my husband is anything but that! He's known in the shadows as the Black Samaritan, the man who helps to save the lives of those trapped in the sex rings here in town."

"Why would he be interested in me, then?"

The silence was deafening as they looked from one to the other. Finally, Tiffany muffled, "Okay, I guess it wouldn't hurt to hear what you have to offer."

Lucy broke into my thoughts. Are you and Sue-Ling ready to head out? We'll see you later, okay?"

Sue-Ling and I said our goodbyes and made our way to the car. I took the bag from Sue-Ling and loaded it into the back seat of my car before coming around to the driver's side. If possible, Sue-Ling seemed to have shrunk in size as she huddled in her place and leaned against the door. I reached over and patted Sue-Ling's hand. "Don't worry. You're in good hands," I said as we pulled out of the driveway and headed north out of Las Vegas.

CHAPTER 3

Less than 60 minutes later, I pulled into the driveway of an old farmhouse tucked back against the mountains, miles from the main road. It was beautiful in its simplicity with white columns and a full wraparound porch. As we came up the walkway, a few loose chickens peered at us but then continued to peck at the ground in search of a stray bug. As we came closer to the house, the hens clucked and scattered, and a big old yellow lab dog knocked against the screen door, pushed it open, and lumbered outside. He gave a single bark in greeting and sniffed at Sue-Ling before making his way to me, his final destination.

I bent and rubbed the dog's ears in greeting. "How are you doing, Scout? Behaving yourself, are you?"

His broad tail whacked my legs as he looked at me with love. I'd rescued him from a man who'd been relentlessly beating him for a minor infraction of his own making. Scout was one of the loves of my life, and my heart lifted each time I saw him. "C'mon, let's join the others," I said to both Scout and Sue-Ling. Laughter came to us from inside the house, and Sue-Ling looked at me with fear showing in her eyes. "C'mon, it's okay. You'll see," I said as I put my arm around Sue-Ling's shoulder and led her forward.

Just then, the door swung open and out charged a small pink-cheeked girl with pigtails. She squealed, "Auntie Tiff!" and ran into my open arms. Then she shyly looked at Sue-Ling, curious. "Who are you?" she asked.

"Sarah, this is Sue-Ling. She's going to be staying here with us for a while."

"Cool," she said and reached for my hand, pulling me forward.

I turned to Sue-Ling. "This is Sarah, Betsy's little girl. Betsy is the one who will be getting your paperwork in order before you move on."

Sue-Ling nodded and tagged along behind. As soon as we stepped through the door, two little Yorkie dogs barked and raced forward, wagging their tails. They began to sniff Sue-Ling, and it was the two of them that brought a genuine smile to Sue-Ling's face. She immediately bent to gather them in her arms as they reached up to lick her face. "Eww, you both are so cute!"

I smiled, pleased. "These two are Frick and Frack." We kept the dogs around and a few other animals that'd come to us for just this reason. They helped to ease a newbie girl into her new situation without judgment of any kind—just love. We knew from experience that the reality of where she was and what lay ahead hadn't fully hit Sue-Ling yet. The next few weeks were going to be tough ones for her, but if she stayed the course, the world would open for many positive things to happen.

I smiled at the three women who stepped forward to greet us. I'd grown to love these women and had learned to trust them with all my heart. These were the ones who completed our "rag-tag" group of girls from the streets who helped others begin a new life. We had come a long way since those early days. By honing our skills, we'd beat the odds of doing what we did without failing to keep our visitors safe. So far, so good. Yes, we were aware that there was always a first time for everything; yet, all we could do is keep our eyes on the ball and not let anything or anyone mess us up. It was hard to believe that nearly eight years had passed since we'd joined together.

"So, what do you have in mind?" Tiffany asked. "Tell me."

Lucy looked at her husband and smiled before she began. "My husband and I want to start something new, and we think you'd be perfect as one of our angels ..."

"Angels?" Tiffany interrupted. "What are you talking about?"

Lester cut in and patted her arm. "Just let her finish,

Tiffany."

Lucy began to explain the fatal shooting of their daughter due to mistaken identity. There had been a large sum of money paid out in a lawsuit, allowing Lester and Lucy to begin life again in a new area—Las Vegas. Their daughter's death had revolved around the mistaken identity of a girl trying to escape her pimp and the business she was in. It had ended badly for both their daughter and the girl; yet, it had instilled a passion in Lester and Lucy to use the death restitution money to help desperate girls escape the rabbit hole that illegal prostitution and sex trafficking created.

Tiffany felt her heart drop as she listened to Lucy. How could she possibly help? She had nothing to offer!

Betsy put her arm around me. "You okay, Tiff? You looked like you were a thousand miles away."

I smiled at Betsy. "I was thinking about how we met. Remember?"

Betsy chortled. "Who could forget? C'mon, let's get Sue-Ling settled in."

Inside, the other angels stood waiting. "I'm Missy, and that's Linda," said Missy as she stepped forward and then pointed at Linda, standing away from them. "We're going to help you settle in. I'll show you to your room, and then you can take a shower and change, okay?"

Sue-Ling lifted her eyes to the staircase. I mouthed the words to Missy. "Keep an eye on her."

She nodded and then turned to Sue-Ling. "My room is right next door to yours. I'll wait for you right there in case you have any questions. C'mon, let's head up, and you little ones can come too," she said to the dogs dancing at Sue-Ling's feet. That seemed to do the trick to encourage Sue-Ling to move forward because she leaned down, grabbed her bag, and headed to the stairs, looking behind her to make sure the dogs were following.

CHAPTER 4

"What's happening?" I asked Linda, who looked excited.

Linda moved closer to where I stood with Betsy. "Come with me into the Bat Room, and I'll show you."

A few months after I'd come to live on the ranch, Linda had shown up at the door. Somehow, she had learned about what we were planning to do. She came to us from the FBI where she'd become disenchanted with her co-workers and the agency's bend to political interference. Also, the FBI had done nothing to help her at a critical time in her life, leaving her no longer believing in the goodness of humans—particularly men.

Linda was a brilliant nerd who had developed her own software to track those involved in illegal sex trafficking, money laundering, drug trafficking, and more. She was a genius, and I was in awe of her abilities to make her way through the internet into various programs and files that were supposed to be foolproof against hacking.

She had come on board to get back at some of the people who'd murdered her best friend after using her for their sexual pleasure. Before they strangled her, they'd laughed and jeered at her pathetic pleas to let her go. In horror, Linda had watched the entire incident as it played out over the internet on one of the many smut and snuff sites she was involved in trying to take down. Devastated and unable to stop what she saw, Linda had screamed in anguish until she had no voice left. Today, her hoarse voice was a constant reminder to anyone who knew her story what she'd endured.

With her tufted hair that changed color nearly every other day and her deep black eyes that glowed with unresolved anger, Linda was intimidating. Despite her appearance, she had a soft heart. However, when on the hunt for offenders exhibiting the same behavior Linda had witnessed with her girlfriend, anyone who got in her way got hurt. She made sure of it.

"Look at this," Linda pointed out to Betsy and me on the computer. "These two pricks are getting ready to set up a 'viewing' of available girls for sale. They've promised it's going to be the biggest and best auction yet—only two weeks away. Time to mess them up, right?"

Betsy and I agreed. One of the problems in today's world was that if someone is accused of doing something terrible, even if they were innocent, there always remains the possibility that what was said might carry some truth. Doubt destroys, and we were going to use that to our advantage as we had in the past. Linda would be able to mount things on the internet to hopefully disturb what those guys were trying to do and cause others to doubt their safety of getting involved.

Betsy put her arm around Linda and me. "Let's nail those bastards, shall we?"

Betsy had been the first angel in place before I came along. She had helped me get through the shame of my having had an abortion and instilled in me that it was my right to choose for both the baby's sake and mine. The abortion was over and done with, and there was nothing I could do about it now. All that encouragement had come from a pregnant woman who didn't know or care who was the father of her child. He was simply one of many men who provided her money, and that's all she wanted from them. She used men for her purpose, and she had no shame with that. She was our financial wizard, and her knowledge about investments had benefited all of us.

I learned that Betsy had been smarter than many of us scraping along in life due to our addictions. She had placed a high price on herself—far more than double the going rate—and had gotten away with it. It was all about the way Betsy had marketed herself, making what she had to offer seem more valuable somehow than the regular sex acts expected. She had set up a "fuck-u" bank account and stashed her money away, wanting a child of her own to love one day. Her olive skin, dark hair, and hazel eyes that snapped with intelligence drew attention, and Betsy was able to choose any man she wanted to use. She didn't have or need a pimp. Having been sexually abused by her own family for years, she'd survived to become stronger, no longer allowing anyone to make choices for her.

I overheard Missy upstairs. "Do you have everything you need for your shower, Sue-Ling?" I smiled. Missy, our fourth angel, had completed several nursing courses to date … mostly through the internet. She had a fascination with hands-on healing and used those higher thoughts of energy to escape into a world of goodness in her mind. The reality of having been a young child involved in a sex trafficking ring for many years far from her loving family was too awful for her to handle. Yet, Missy was the one who comforted the new girls and gave them hope that their world could become peaceful and loving. We hid as much as we could of the seamier side of what we were doing from her, not wanting to taint her optimism. Although strong physically, Missy was tender in ways that demonstrated the mind's ability to coat the truth and bend it to what one was able to endure. Not aware of the extent of her importance, Missy was the one who, by merely being her loving self, kept us all grounded and in better balance. If we were feeling down, we sought out Missy's touch and support. With her long blond hair, light blue eyes, and petite body, she resembled an angel, one we all wanted to be around.

I thought back to the time I'd been asked to become one of the angels.

"Why would you be interested in me?" Tiffany asked.

"You have a resilience that's necessary to survive. I've watched you these past weeks when you've come into the soup kitchen to catch a meal. I think you're a gambler at heart just like any good entrepreneur. I think you've got what it takes to make a success of yourself —just in a different way," explained Lester.

"I don't know," she said as doubt filled her.

"You'll never know unless you try, will you?" asked Lester.

Beginning to understand she didn't have many options open to her, Tiffany asked, "Where will I live? What do I need to do?"

"First, you need to rest and heal. Then, after you detox and it's time for you to leave the hospital, we'll talk some more. You need to trust us. Can you do that?" asked Lucy.

Looking into Lucy's chocolate eyes, Tiffany nodded and felt a weight of worry lifted. She intuitively knew that as long as Lucy was close by her, she was safe. It was a feeling that spread across her body with a certainty that stayed with her.

"Auntie Tiff? You're not listening to me!"

I chuckled at Sarah's stance—legs spread and arms crossed—and a pretend scowl that broke as soon as she heard me laugh. "It's time to collect the eggs, Auntie

25

Tiff, and I'm afraid of the rooster. Can you please help me?"

"Of course, pip-squeak, let's go!

"I'm not a pip-squeak! I'm seven!"

"I know. I apologize for calling you that, Madame," I said, bowing before her and kissing her hand.

Giggles erupted before Sarah flung herself into my arms. "I love you, Auntie Tiff!"

"I love you too," I murmured into her wiry hair. If only you knew how much, I thought. My being a part of Sarah's life had pushed me to do all that I could to be the best I could be. In many ways, she was my little savior.

Missy descended the stairs. "Are Lester and Sarah joining us for dinner?"

"Yes," I said.

"Good. I made plenty of stew this morning, so we should have more than enough food. How are you, Tiff?"

"Everything is fine. And you? How are you doing?"

"Now that we've got another girl to push through, I'll be busy, which is always good. I hate sitting around."

"Nobody can accuse you of sitting around with all the projects you've got going on with your knitting for charity and taking care of the animals and the rest of us."

"True," Missy smiled. "You girls give me such a hard time with all your demands," she teased,

26

knowing things were pretty easy-going around there at the ranch without any mishaps.

CHAPTER 5

When Lester and Lucy arrived, I pulled Lester aside. I was still uncomfortable about Sue-Ling joining us, and I didn't know why, but I felt I had to discuss my feelings with Lester. "Can you tell me more about Sue-Ling?"

Lester held his head in his hands as he sat with his elbows on his knees. "Well, I don't know that much about her. One of the volunteers at the soup kitchen came to me. He said there was a girl out front who'd said she needed help or someone was going to kill her."

My heart pumped faster. So Sue-Ling had not come through the regular channels then. Usually, Lester received a call from one of the non-profits in town, who dealt with addictions or human trafficking, saying they'd had no luck in finding space in one of their safe houses and needed his help. They knew he had a safe house somewhere, but didn't know where. Many thought it was in Pahrump, a small town outside of Las Vegas.

Although it was well-known that the soup kitchen was owned and run by Lucy and Lester, no one knew about our "angel" house. And it was vital that our secrecy remain or the whole safety thing could blow up in our face. "Why did you go off course with this one, Lester?"

"I've been asking myself that same question, and I don't know the answer. Lucy isn't happy with me, either," he added with a sigh.

"Well, we're going to have to be careful. As you know, there are new gangs here from Asia competing with the Mexican gangs, and, frankly, it's a mess. It's odd, too, Lester, that Sue-Ling already had a suitcase packed, ready to go. Most times, there is no planning ahead. It's usually a quick escape."

"So what do you think we should do?" he asked.

"In my sessions with her, I'll try to find out if anything is going on that could come back and bite us. With any girl that comes through here, there's always some danger of retaliation from the pimps should they discover us. I'm pretty sure she doesn't' know this area out here, and thank God, the ranch is so isolated that unless you knew your way here, you wouldn't be able to find it."

"Well, that's something good, isn't it?"

"Papa? Where are you?" Sarah's smiling face peeked into the room where we sat, and her eyes lit up when she saw Lester. His face brightened. He loved the role of being her grandfather, and his pride in her showed on his face.

He waved her into the room to his side. "Auntie Tiff and I were talking. What have you been up to, squirt?"

"I'm not a squirt, and I'm not a pip-squeak like Auntie Tiff said either, Papa. I'm seven now."

Lester chuckled. "I'm going to have to remember that, aren't I?"

"Yes, Papa, you are," she warned.

Lester and I both laughed, knowing that the ranch without Sarah would be pretty dull. "Let's just keep a careful eye on things, okay?" said Lester.

"I have a feeling we'll need to," I responded. "I'll let the other girls know too."

"C'mon, Missy says it's time to eat," ordered Sarah, pulling on Lester.

We sat around the large, maple farmer's table and held hands as Lester said grace. Missy served each of us a bowl of her stew and passed around a large tossed salad she'd made with fresh vegetables from the garden. It was apparent that Sue-Ling was uncomfortable in our midst. She only picked at her food and kept her head down. Lester rested his hand on her shoulder and leaned into her. "Are you okay, Sue-Ling?"

Her eyes watered, and she nodded her head. We looked at each other and remained silent because we remembered what it had been like our first night here. It was a big adjustment, and not everyone was up for it. Again, my worry about Sue-Ling flashed across my mind.

Missy said, "Not to worry, Sue-Ling. You're among friends, and you'll soon settle in before you know it."

I remembered my first night at the ranch; it'd been frightening.

"Where is this place you're taking me? There's nothing out here!"

Lucy patted her shoulder. "It's okay, Tiffany, you'll see."

"Are you sure you're on the right road?" she asked.

Lester chuckled and kept on driving. He rounded a bend, and hidden between some tall pine trees was a narrow, paved road that led them closer to the mountain. Further on, she was able to make out her first view of the three-story house with its white pillars and wrap-around porch. It was beautiful, and she felt an odd peace come over her.

When they got there, she climbed out of the car and grabbed her small suitcase. She'd packed just her essentials and several changes of clothes that she'd picked out at the Salvation Army store. An attractive girl about her age waddled forward and introduced herself as Betsy. Seeing her pregnant, Tiffany felt the loss of her baby—at her own hand. All Tiffany wanted at that point was a tall glass of vodka and maybe a sniff of coke. The hospital had helped her through the first 28 days of detoxing, and that'd been hell. Getting straight was not for the weak, and at that moment, given the right circumstances, Tiffany would have chosen to go back into that rabbit hole.

Betsy seemed aware of Tiffany's turmoil, and she

grabbed her hand like a mother reaching for her child in a protective mode. She led her into the house. "I'll show you your room. It's right next door to mine."

"Dessert, anyone?" asked Missy. "I made an apple tart, especially for you, Sue-Ling."

"Missy, I want a piece. Can I have ice cream, too?" asked Sarah.

"Finish your salad first; then you can have dessert," said Betsy.

"Okay, Momma. You'd better finish your salad, too, Sue-Ling," added Sarah, eying Sue-Ling's nearly full plate.

We laughed, including Sue-Ling. Good, I thought, she's going to be alright.

CHAPTER 6

After Lester and Lucy left, Missy took Sue-Ling with her to show her the nighttime routine to secure the animals from the coyotes that wandered the mountains. The barn had an attached hen house where they'd tuck in the few hens that remained around the house. Inside the barn were two horses to be fed and two cows to be milked.

After tucking Sarah into bed, Betsy joined Linda and me to lay out the plan to take down and disable the men who were planning to auction off the girls they were displaying on their website. We had learned the hard way to fight a fair fight, we had to do things on the same level as the ones we were trying to take down. That meant we had to take risks and do some things illegally.

Thanks to Linda's expertise with writing code for the computer, she had devised a way to get into the predator's bank account and deplete it of its large amount of money. Linda then transferred it to an exclusive off-shore account. From there, she broke up the stolen money into smaller amounts and wire-transferred them to various pass-through bank accounts that couldn't be traced. The funds ultimately ended up in a joint bank account we owned. So far, the two times we'd stolen money, we'd gotten away with it. After the second time, we came clean with Lester and Lucy, who were against what we'd done, saying we were tempting fate. Karma wasn't always kind, so there were other ways of getting even they said—like sending the predators to jail. Anyone sent to prison for sex trafficking usually didn't survive very well.

For each of the two times that we'd stolen money, chaos had developed between the predators themselves, with everyone involved accusing the other of the theft, and they began to self-destruct. Then we, and our silent partner working at the FBI were able to leak information to the special task force covering human trafficking and take down the villains.

Betsy, being the one who handled the finances, invested the monies we'd stolen. She set up an account using part of the funds as a base to financially help the young girls and women escaping human trafficking get a new start in life. We allowed ourselves a small percentage of the stolen money that we invested and held in individual accounts. Not quite the 'Robin Hood' of the past—more like women helping women.

It was Lucy and Lester who kept their non-profit organization going. They made donations to several of the non-profits across the country that helped provide safe housing for the girls who came through the ranch looking for a way out of the mess they were in, caught with nowhere else to go.

I looked to Linda, who was bent over her computer, fingers flying across the keyboard. My thoughts flew to the time we'd first met.

When Linda joined Betsy and Tiffany a few months later, Tiffany wasn't sure she could trust her. She was short and rough-looking with spiked hair dyed various colors, tattoos on her body, and a nose ring that reminded her of one of her children's books picturing a pig with a ring in its nose. Her voice was rough, sounding hoarse, and her demeanor gave off the impression that she'd take no hostages.

In the beginning, Tiffany was uncomfortable around her and tried to stay as far away from her as possible. One night, after each of them had gone their separate ways, Tiffany changed her mind about reading and decided to check on the new foal. The light was on in the barn, and as Tiffany got closer to it, she thought she heard someone crying. She stealthily made her way inside to see Linda huddled next to the foal, stroking its neck, tears rolling down her face. "Being here with you makes me believe that not all things are bad." She sniffled. "What happened to my friend is not the way it's supposed to be, is it? I promise you that I'll make them and anyone like them pay. I'll do everything I can to make it a better world for you and everyone else."

Tiffany quietly retraced her steps back to the house, reflecting on what she'd seen. It was then that she expanded her heart to include Linda. From that night on, she and Linda grew closer with each new day and ended up as close as any two sisters could be.

I heard Missy outside, making clucking sounds to get the hens into the hen house. My thoughts turned to her.

A few weeks later, Lucy brought Missy into their circle, and she became the "mother" to all of them, representing the mother she had never had. It was her way of coping after a horrendous abduction, multiple rapes, and starvation. She made the world around her become a loving one, blocking out all the bad. She refused to look back; otherwise, she wouldn't survive.

Lucy and Lester referred to the four of us as their "angels out of the dark," something none of us took lightly, knowing we were far from the angels of the heavens.

"I'm ready to call in Jerome to work with us, okay?" asked Linda.

Betsy and I nodded. "Have you kept him up to date so far?" I asked.

Linda looked at me and winked. "Damn straight."

"Good," Betsy said. "Let's see what he has to say."

Jerome used to work side by side with Linda at the FBI, as much a tech geek as she was. Although he was as unhappy as Linda had been working there, he had promised Linda that he'd help her bring down the men who had murdered her girlfriend. The best way for

Jerome to do that was by his remaining at the FBI, where he had access to all kinds of information available at his fingertips. Although they hadn't been able to bring down those involved in what had happened to Linda's girlfriend so far, he unofficially signed on with us to continue our private work to assist girls out of their rabbit holes. In actuality, it meant we were working with the FBI, albeit in secrecy.

I'd only met Jerome once, and he looked nothing like I'd imagined. Instead of looking like the consummate FBI detective—someone tall in a dark blue suit and a button-down shirt—he wore jeans and a tee-shirt with a beach scene and the words "Don't bother me; I'm on vacation" scrawled across it. He was the perfect person to be helping us at the FBI without drawing attention. It wasn't until he removed his signature sunglasses that his magnificent sparkling blue eyes became visible and shone with intelligence and humor. I immediately liked him, and intuitively felt that we could trust him.

I thought Linda had a crush on him, which was odd since she openly didn't trust any man. But maybe it was because they worked so closely and well together. But nothing was said about it.

"Hey, boo," Jerome said. "What's up?" he asked over the speakerphone.

"Hi Jer, what did you find out?" Linda asked.

"The FBI has been trailing your guys and is looking to bust them wide open. However, they haven't been able to figure out where this auction is going to take place. Any ideas?"

"From what I've been able to trace, they are broadcasting from a different location each time they advertise the auction. I'm beginning to see a pattern, though. Here, log into my computer, and I'll show you what I mean."

I left them to do their thing and hoped that soon they'd come up with something to tip-off the task force. It was interesting that in all the years we'd been giving the task force clues, they had no idea we were involved. We had Linda and Jerome to thank for that.

I said goodnight to Betsy, Missy, and Sue-Ling and climbed the stairs to my bedroom at the top of the house. I loved my attic space that had skylights and French doors that opened onto a private deck at one end. It was my bit of heaven when I needed it to be. It was where I allowed myself the time and space to contemplate the past, present, and future. Although I didn't allow myself to wallow in the past because that did no good, I used those thoughts to put perspective on my choices of the day.

I felt queasy in a way that'd in the past meant that significant changes were about to happen. I had no idea what that might mean. I just knew they were on the way.

CHAPTER 7

I awoke the next morning with a heaviness that hadn't been there the day before. I tried to put my finger on what was causing that feeling, and then remembered we had a new girl here—Sue-Ling. I'd have my first session with her before I headed back to town to meet with my scheduled clients for today. Sometimes, it was hard for me to believe that I was a trained therapist. I had come close to not having that come about:

> "You want me to do what?" Tiffany asked in dismay.
> "Go back to school and earn your degree. It won't be that difficult because you can take courses over the internet now."
> "A degree in what?" she asked, perplexed.
> "A Bachelor of Social Work."

"Are you kidding? I can't do that!" Tiffany replied, upset.

"Why not?" asked Lester. "Four years will fly by, and you'll have something at the end to show for yourself."

"What do I need that for?" she scoffed.

Lester remained silent, making Tiffany uncomfortable. After a long pause, he asked, "What do you think you'd do with that knowledge?"

Tiffany knew what he wanted her to say, but she didn't respond. How could she? Yes, she'd like to help others who had suffered her shame, but she couldn't take the chance of failing. If she failed again at anything, she didn't think she'd be able to rally.

"Well?" prodded Lester.

"I'm sorry, Lester, but I can't do it."

"Think about it. Remember, whatever you learn is yours to do with whatever you want. There's no right or wrong, you know. There's only perspective, and sometimes that's all people need to be reminded of to know they have value no matter what has happened to them."

She became lost in his words. "Leave me the paperwork," she ordered, grumpily. "I'll look it over and let you know, okay?"

I showered and put on clean clothes that were part of the wardrobe I left at the ranch. Missy would take my dirty ones from the hamper like she usually did and have them washed and ready for me the next time I came out. As much as I'd insisted I could take care of my own laundry, Missy was equally insistent that it was her job. I rather liked being spoiled that way, and I made sure to thank her every time she did that for me.

As I descended the stairs, I smelled coffee brewing and bacon cooking. I smiled. God bless Missy! I walked into the kitchen to find Sarah sitting at the table in her nightgown, sipping cocoa. I fluffed her hair as I walked by to pour myself a cup of coffee and grab a piece of cooked bacon. "Good morning!" I said to Betsy and Linda, who had just wandered into the kitchen. "Where's Missy and Sue-Ling?"

Betsy and Linda chuckled. "Missy had Sue-Ling up at the break of dawn, out milking the cows before she knew what'd hit her," said Linda in her croaky voice.

I laughed. Missy had the right idea to keep Sue-Ling so busy she couldn't think about anything but what she was doing. We heard Sue-Ling's high-pitched voice coming nearer. "You mean we have to clean the stalls every day?"

"Yup," came Missy's response. "C'mon, let's grab some breakfast before you meet with Tiffany, okay?"

The screen door banged open, and the rest of us smiled as Missy and Sue-Ling carried in their pals of fresh milk. "Put it right there," said Missy, pointing to the counter and I'll strain it. I'm going to churn this into butter. You can help me later."

"Good morning!" I said.

Missy smiled broadly. "It's a beautiful morning, isn't it, Sue-Ling?"

Sue-Ling nodded with much less enthusiasm than Missy.

"I'll fix the eggs. Who wants what?" I asked.

After I doled out the fried eggs, we all joined Sarah, who was still sitting at the table, sipping her cocoa. It was interesting to watch Sue-Ling dive into her breakfast after laboring in the barn. I looked at Betsy, who raised her brow in acknowledgment that she'd noticed too. Linda winked at us, and Missy smiled.

After we cleared the table, I said. "Ready, Sue-Ling? Let's go into the office so we can have some privacy."

The office was tucked away in the back part of the house, and when Sue-Ling entered, she headed to the large, puffy wingback chair. She curled up in the comfy chair and moved into its corner as if to hide while I sat behind the desk to make our talk seem more like a professional session. "I'm going to ask you some simple questions, and then I'll answer any questions you have for me, okay?"

Sue-Ling nodded dully.

"Where were you born?"

"Los Angeles, California," she mumbled.

"How old are you?"

"Eighteen."

"Are your parents alive? If so, are they still living in Los Angeles?"

"My mother is there, but my father passed away when I was little. I don't remember him," she said in a tiny voice.

"Did your mother ever re-marry?"

"No. My mother, my brother, and I moved in with my uncle," she whispered with a sigh, obviously not happy about it.

"Ahh." That would be something to touch on later. Many foreigners expanded their family to include other relatives. "What brought you to Las Vegas?"

"He promised me I could be a dancer and make lots of money ..." Her voice trailed off.

"So, who was this man who promised you that, Sue-Ling?"

"You're not going to let him know where I am, are you? He'll kill me!"

"No, I'm not," I firmly stated.

The thing I noticed when Sue-Ling began her story was that she didn't seem angry or determined enough to make the switch to start a new life. That worried me. It was like for some of us addicts—we need to hit bottom before we decide enough is enough. I thought of Anais Nin's quote I often used with my clients – "And the day came when the risk to remain tight in a bud was more painful than the risk it took to blossom." I observed her when she spoke.

"My boyfriend," she mumbled. Her face flushed with a sudden joy before dropping as the realization of what that meant—leaving her sitting before me.

"So, how are you feeling right now? A little confused?"

Sue-Ling raised her head and stared at me without a word.

"It's not your fault, you know," I stated.

"What do you mean?" she demanded in anger.

"For wanting more in your life—a better life."

Sue-Ling's face heated. "That's easy for you to say," she said in disgust.

"It's not always easy to talk about it, is it? I know that's how it worked for me."

Sue-Ling looked at me in surprise. "You?"

"Yes, everyone here has pretty much gone through something like you have. So we know how difficult it can be."

Sue-Ling bent her head down. "Ohh ..."

"I want to make something clear to you in case you didn't understand. I'm only here talking to you to get you started on your journey to heal and change your lifestyle. When we feel you're ready, we'll move you along to the next stop. Did Lester explain that to you?"

Sue-Ling nodded, not looking up.

"Any questions for me?"

Sue-Ling remained still.

"I'll return here tonight for the weekend. We'll talk then, okay?"

Sue-Ling stared at me, not saying a word. I stood up, patted her head on my way out, and hurried to my car to drive back to Vegas. I didn't want to be late for my first client.

CHAPTER 8

Driving back to town, I let my mind wander. Although I had my doubts about Sue-Ling, I needed to befriend her—encourage her, and be willing to support her on her journey without giving up on her— as Lester and Lucy had done for me.

"I'm glad you changed your mind, Tiffany. Wait and see. You're going to be so good at this; I know you are. Let's sign you up for classes right now."

Tiffany felt sick. Wonder if she failed? Why was she letting the consummate people pleaser part of her take over? Isn't that how she had fallen into the trap of sex and drugs? The worried expression on Lester's face jarred her from her thoughts. "Oh no, are you having second thoughts about doing this?" she asked, unnerved. "You don't think I can do it, do you?"

He immediately reached out and patted her arm. "It

doesn't matter what I think, does it? What do you think about it all, Tiffany? Think long and hard about it for a moment. How would earning this degree make you feel as a person?"

Without thought, she blurted out, "That I'm more than a pretty face, and what I have to say matters... that I do so count for something in this fucking world!" She felt the heat in her face rise as tears filled her eyes.

Lester smiled at her. "That says it all, doesn't it? Let's go and sign you up for your classes."

Despite what they'd said, I had no idea why Lester and Lucy had chosen me as one of their lucky ones to be part of their family. What I'd come to learn is that, yes, indeed, there are real-life earth angels, and they were two of them. They helped others and stood by them no matter what, and I needed to be there for Sue-Ling in the same way, I scolded myself.

The morning flew by with no surprises. My Friday afternoon schedule was always light, so before too long, I gathered my things together and headed out to the ranch for the weekend. I felt a flutter in my stomach as I drove closer, which quickly expanded into a panic when I saw Missy, Betsy, and Linda spread out about the ranch calling Sue-Ling's name. Sarah came running from the back of the house with the little dogs barking at her feet. "She's over there!" she yelled, pointing behind her.

I parked the car, hopped out, and ran to where they surrounded Sue-Ling's prone figure. Her eyes were rolled back in her head, but she was still breathing. I bent and felt her pulse, which was beating a slow, steady pace. I lifted her arm to get a closer look and saw fresh needle marks. "Damn it!" I shouted. "How did she get this past us?" We looked at each other and shook our heads. I bent over her. "She's going to be okay if she makes it through the hell of detoxing. Luckily we have the meds to ease her down until we can get her into a good place."

Missy immediately rushed forward and bent down to Sue-Ling's side and pushed her damp hair away from her face. "Let's lift her inside. We'll put her in the guest room downstairs for the night."

"Wait! I'll get the stretcher," said Betsy as she took hold of Sarah's hand and led her away. Sarah was calm, having been exposed to this before, which made her declare on many occasions that she intended to become a nurse when she grew up. The resiliency of that child amazed me.

"It's going to be a rough night," Linda whispered to me by my side.

"Yeah, I agree. Let's hope we can straighten out Sue-Ling in record time. Do you know what happened?"

"Sue-Ling told Missy she had to go to the bathroom, and then she didn't come back right away, and Missy put out the call for us to find her."

"The usual then," I said. "It's been a while since we've had anyone here, so it's easy to understand how we've become slack to possible warnings. How is the other mess going, Linda?"

"We're pretty sure we've identified one of the men involved. Jerome and I think we might be able to break into his bank account easily enough, but the problem is getting worse because we're finding that these perverts don't always bank their money, preferring to keep their cash on hand."

"Damn. Removing the perps' money seems to be the most effective way of getting back at them," I said.

"It's the most fun, anyhow," confirmed Linda.

Betsy returned with the stretcher, and we hoisted Sue-Ling onto it and carried her inside. As we lifted her onto the bed, she began to stir, and her eyes fluttered open and widened when she saw the four of us hovering over her. She began to moan and turned her head away. Missy grabbed her hand and held onto it. "We'll get through this together, Sue-Ling. Don't you worry; you won't have to do this alone."

The guest room where Sue-Ling lay was bare of anything non-essential. She was not the only one to be there. There'd been a few girls who'd come through the ranch who'd ended up in the room and had suffered in it. Getting sober and clean was not for the weak.

I tried to push away any anger over the fact that we hadn't stuck to the rules of who we allowed to be with us at the ranch. Getting angry was not going to help anyone. "Alright, Missy, you make up the schedule, and we'll take turns staying here with Sue-Ling."

"You look upset, Tiff," said Betsy.

"I just have a funny feeling that we're in for a lot of trouble with this one. I want to make sure she doesn't ruin what we have going on here."

Betsy's brow furrowed. "Yes, we need to be careful and not let her out of our sight. We can't trust her for a second."

Linda rushed from the room to answer her phone that she'd left in the Bat Room. Betsy and I followed her and stepped closer when her voice raised in tone and volume. "Here? Right now?"

She looked at us and flapped her hand, signaling us to remain quiet. "The timing couldn't be worst. Let me ask them. Hold on." Linda's face fell. "You're not going to believe this. The FBI is questioning Jerome about his work, accusing him of illegal searches. They've given him a leave of absence until they can figure out if he's involved in something nefarious. He's wondering if he can hide out here for a few days. He'll be able to help me make the moves we need to make to bring down the internet predators."

Betsy and I looked at each other, silently questioning one another. We came to the same conclusion at the same time. "Yes," we echoed.

I watched Linda's darkened face light up as she took in that Jerome would be around, working with her. "The girls say, yes, but that you have to be especially nice to me," she said as she winked at us.

We laughed and wondered what it'd mean to have him here, and how that was going to work out in the long haul.

CHAPTER 9

It was impossible not to hear Sue-Ling's groans as she struggled to free herself from Missy's insistence that she remain in bed. We smiled at each other as we heard Missy lower her voice and speak in unladylike terms. "Listen here, bitch, you need to do as I say."

She'd learned that if she spoke roughly as the pimps did, those in a drugged fog would more likely obey her command. Although she hated talking like that, Missy knew how important it was that Sue-Ling remain where she was. She softened her stance. "You'll be fine; just trust me," she added as she gave Sue-Ling an approved sedative for someone in her condition.

I smiled to myself. Missy was a marvel. I went into the living room to see Sarah sitting on the couch with her headset on listening to an audiobook. Sarah was oblivious to what was happening around her, intent on listening with her finger trailing along the written words of the book. Betsy handled Sarah in such a loving manner and calming ease that Sarah was remarkably well-adjusted despite some of her exposure to the visitors who came through the ranch.

Heavy footsteps sounded on the porch. Then the doorbell rang, causing Sarah to abdicate her reading and race to the door. She looked at her mother in surprise. "It's a man," she announced as if he were the oddity he was.

Linda came rushing forward. "Hi, Jerome, c'mon in."

"Hi, boo. Where do you want me to park this?" he asked, tipping his head at the suitcase at his feet.

"Just leave it there. You'll be staying in the shed. Is that okay?"

"Shed?" he asked in confusion.

"The guest house in the back," she said as she lightly punched his arm. "It's nice; you'll see."

Missy walked in to see who'd come. Linda filled Missy in on why Jerome was here. I decided to take over Missy's night of cooking. "Missy, I've got dinner covered. I'm going to grill chicken outside. Is everyone okay with that?" I asked.

Betsy piped up, "You'd better put on extra chicken for Jerome. I'll set the table."

"Right on," I responded as I headed to the kitchen. I smiled to myself, knowing whatever I fixed for dinner would be better than the first time I had been in charge of putting together a meal at the ranch.

"My turn to cook? Are you sure you want me to cook? Tiffany asked.

"Tiffany, we all have to take turns, you know," said Betsy, "and tonight it's your turn."

"Okay, as long as you know, I don't have much practice."

"You'll do fine," encouraged Missy while Linda held her tongue.

She went into the kitchen and opened the essential cookbook that Missy handed her. And because the picture looked so pretty, she turned to the recipe for roast chicken. Then, she pulled out a whole chicken from the freezer and followed the instructions for stuffing. An hour later, the bird was stuffed and put into the oven. The string beans were out of the cans, ready to be heated. As Tiffany was finishing her clean-up, Missy came into the kitchen and asked if she needed any help. Tiffany smugly answered, "Nope. All set."

"Good. We're all starving. What are you fixing?"

She'd answered, "Roast chicken!"

"Really?" Missy asked. "I don't smell anything cooking."

Tiffany stood there with her mouth open. "I put the chicken into the oven. I wonder what went wrong."

Missy shook her head as she went to the oven and opened the door to see the pan of frozen chicken sitting inside. "How about turning the oven on?" she'd laughed.

That night they'd ended up eating pizza, and the following night they'd eaten the roast chicken. Since then, Tiffany had become the champion of the outdoor grill.

I laughed at the memory and went outside to start the grill.

Later, as we slipped into our seats at the table, Jerome and Linda were the last to be seated. Both looked worried. "What's up?" I asked.

"Nothing good," answered Jerome, looking at Linda for confirmation. "We're not sure what the FBI will find on my desk computer—the one they confiscated. Anything that might lead to you all, I put it into a hidden folder. Even if they do find it, I don't think they'll be able to break into it. But I need to warn you all to be careful, especially you, Tiffany. You're the one living in town and traveling back and forth."

"We can't let that stop us, right?" asked Linda.

We all nodded in agreement.

After dinner, it was my turn to sit with Sue-Ling, who was still sleeping. While I sat there in the lounge chair tipped back, Sarah joined me with a book clasped in her hand. I patted the space next to me, and she crawled into my lap. "Hi, baby, do you want to read the book to me?"

A smile broke across her face, and she nodded as she wriggled beside me. I rested my head back and closed my eyes. Her sweet voice surrounded me like a "thumb" blanket small children use for comfort. Soon, I felt myself nod off. I woke up to hear the rustling of the covers on Sue-Ling's bed as she squirmed. Sarah was gone, and it was dark outside. I got up and went to Sue-Ling's bed and touched her forehead. It was hot, too hot. I saw the raised swelling around the pin pick on her arm. I quickly left to get Missy.

Together, we took turns with iced washcloths to cool Sue-Ling down. After several long hours, her fever broke, and Missy and I looked at each other, relief on our faces. Missy applied more antibiotic cream onto Sue-Ling's arm to further fight the infection.

Before morning, Betsy came to relieve us, and Missy and I headed to bed to catch a few hours of sleep. My heart lurched when I thought of all that was going wrong.

Later that night, a bedraggled Sue-Ling joined us for dinner. She looked pathetic as she poked at her food, too embarrassed to look up from her full plate. Even Sarah quietly watched her. Jerome seemed surprised to see her there because he hadn't known she was in the house. "So, what's your name?" he asked.

Sue-Ling remained quiet.

Missy spoke up, "This is Sue-Ling. She's staying with us for a while. Sue-Ling, this is Jerome. He's here to work with Linda."

At that, Sue-Ling looked up and studied him, but again said nothing.

"We have chores to do after dinner, Sue-Ling, so eat up," Missy said as she patted her on the back.

"Can I help, too?" asked Sarah.

"Sure," agreed Missy after a slight nod from Betsy.

After dinner, I headed to the barn to saddle up Big Red, the larger of the two horses. "C'mon, girl, let's take a ride." I needed to get away and let my thoughts race with the wind and clear my head. I'd head back to the city tomorrow earlier than usual. I knew from experience that nothing was sacred to the FBI, especially privacy, and they'd do everything possible to learn what Jerome was doing and who was involved. I needed to be extra cautious and alert to anyone new around me. I'd have to take different backroads out of town. You never knew.

The next morning, I met with Sue-Ling after her chores. She was a different person from the first time we'd met. It was obvious she was depressed and angry.

"How are you feeling, Sue-Ling?" I asked.

"How do you think?" she asked in a surly voice.

"I imagine not so good. So, let's start from the beginning. Why did you agree to come here?"

"Why do you think? He was going kill me, you know!" she spat out, furious.

"Yes, I do know, and I can guess it was because you weren't bringing in enough money, right?"

Sue-Ling stared at me. "So now that I've fucked up, I'm outta here, right?" she asked defiantly.

"No, but you are going to have to change your ways. Lester explained how your coming here works; I know he did. So there are no surprises. You have other people here to consider whether you like it or not."

"You're all so nice and goody, goody. I can't do it. I'd rather take my chances back on the street."

I laughed, which surprised her. "Quite a change from where you've been to here, isn't it? Don't you worry; you'll get used to all the niceness."

58

"So what happens now?" she asked, curious.

"You're not the only one to slip up, you know. The secret is to keep your eye on your goal. That is if your goal is to be clean and sober. Haven't you secretly wanted to do something different but believed that you couldn't? You'd be surprised how being clean and sober can bring miracles into your life. You're allowed to dream, Sue-Ling. You just have to want it badly enough."

"Wonder if I can't do it?"

"You'll never know unless you try. I know it's not easy, but I can tell you it's worth the effort. Stop judging yourself. Just take one hour at a time, and keep busy!"

"So, how come you're not staying?"

"I've got my practice in town. But I'll be back in a day or two to check up on you. Make sure you attend the AA meetings here twice a day with Missy, Betsy, and Linda. Any questions?"

"No," she sighed.

"Sue-Ling, I have a favor to ask of you. Will you look after the dogs? That's my job when I'm here, but I'll need you to do it when I'm not here. Sarah can help too, okay?" She seemed to perk up at that.

I'd learned that it was good for me to ask for a favor because it was an excellent way to get that person to feel good about taking on that responsibility and succeed in doing it. "You're a smart girl, and I know you'll be able to turn your life around. I believe in you. See you soon." I stood up and hugged her despite her holding herself away from me. Then, I took off.

CHAPTER 10

Driving back to the city, I was distracted and came close to hitting the car in front of me when it suddenly stopped. I was rewarded with a raised finger out of the driver's window. I mouthed, "Sorry," but he lifted his finger again and sped away.

I sighed. What would we do if the FBI discovered what we've been up to these past years? I needed to fill in Lester and Lucy to what was going on. Maybe they'd know the best way to handle it if it ever came to that.

I turned off the main road and wound my way to their house. They lived simply in the house where Lucy grew up. It was a nicely kept, cozy stucco ranch house, typical of most in the valley. I pulled into their driveway behind Lucy's car, and before I could even get out of the vehicle, the front door sprung open, and Lucy's smiling face appeared. My heart lifted as it did each time I saw her. "Hey, baby, what's up?" she asked as she waved me inside.

After I climbed the stairs and began to pass her to enter the house, she pulled me back into a welcoming hug with her beautiful brown face crinkled in smiles. "You know, I'm not going to let you get away without a hug, don't you?" she laughed, and I chuckled with her, appreciating our friendship even more.

As I stepped away from her, she studied me and frowned. "Trouble in paradise?"

"I'm afraid so."

"C'mon in and tell us about it, okay? Lester should be home any minute now."

As I relayed my concerns to both of them, they looked at each other, silently communing their common worry. Finally, Lester spoke. "We've always known the possibility of what we're doing might come to the forefront. Taking in girls from their pimps and moving them along to various rehabs and safe houses is not a problem as long as we protect ourselves by having them sign releases and the other proper papers our lawyer has advised. Legally, we're doing nothing wrong unless one of the girls accuses us of something unforeseen, and that doesn't seem likely with what we have in place."

"We girls don't want anything to disrupt what you are doing for others. It's such a gift. I know what it's meant to me."

Lucy stepped forward and patted me on the shoulder. "Why don't we take it one day at a time, okay?"

"I'm sorry about Sue-Ling's relapse. Do you think you'll be able to straighten her out enough to be able to move her along?" asked Lester.

"With the four of us working together, I think so," I answered, silently praying that was true. Time would tell.

"Are you sure you don't want to stay for dinner?" asked Lucy. "We've plenty of food."

"No, I need to get home. I have my weekly chores to do that I didn't do Friday. I need to begin the week fresh."

I drove to my one-story house in the older section of Las Vegas, where many lawyers had their offices. It was a pretty bungalow house with an old-fashioned front porch and a green grass lawn in front and back. I loved it.

I walked back from my detached garage and entered the house from the front. At the foot of the opened door, I picked up the mail splayed on the floor. I smiled as I always did each time I stepped inside to see its beauty. When I first owned it, everything was gutted inside to make it open and spacious. So with the front door open, it looked like one massive room with a living room, dining area, and updated kitchen open and airy with skylights. Just beyond the kitchen, the laundry room and powder room sat tucked in. The wall at the rear held a hidden doorway that opened to two large master suites with updated bathrooms, one with a modern walk-in shower, the other with a whirlpool bathtub. Anyone who entered the house quickly became overwhelmed by its pure splendor.

My office was attached to the house with a separate entrance. Except for what looked like a closet door, it was not noticeable from the inside.

I loved coming home and be reminded of how far I've come from that day Lester found me on the street.

A wave of cool air blew across me, causing goosebumps to cover my body. Although everyone has psychic abilities, I'd learn to pay close attention to mine, and that was a warning. I checked my windows and back door to make sure all was secure.

After changing my bed sheets and bath towels, I tossed the dirty ones in the laundry and began to vacuum. I nearly missed the ringing doorbell. I wearily went to answer it, and there was a small Asian man on the other side of my safety screen. "You meet with me now?" he asked.

"I'm sorry, but my office is closed for the day. You'll have to come back tomorrow."

"You no meet with me now?"

"I'm so sorry, but you'll have to come back tomorrow," I repeated as I started to close the door.

"I want know Sue-Ling safe."

My heart thudded. "What did you say?"

"Where Sue-Ling?"

"I don't know who you're talking about; why do you think I know?"

"Lady said Sue-Ling come here."

"I'm sorry, but I don't know any Sue-Ling. What's your name, and who sent you?"

The man's hunched shoulders lowered in defeat, and he shook his head, not acknowledging either name. "You tell Sue-Ling I here?" he asked hopefully.

"I'm so sorry, but I don't know Sue-Ling," I repeated emphatically. "What's your name?"

"Tell Sue-Ling come home," and he left and disappeared before I could unfasten the lock on the door and step out.

Who had set him up to contact me? Time to call the girls and let them know what'd happened.

CHAPTER 11

By the time my first client showed up, I was a wreck. I hadn't slept well, and my nerves were shot, putting me on edge. When I opened the door to let my client in, I drew her attention when I leaned forward and scouted the area outside. I had the nagging worry that something unforeseen was going to happen.

"What's the matter? Is everything all right?" she asked, nervously.

"Yes, of course," I answered with a forced calmness and a smile. "C'mon in."

Time passed, and after the third client, I took a break and made myself a cup of mint tea. I leaned back in my swivel chair with my feet on top of the desk, knowing my last client for the day wasn't for another hour. I closed my eyes and began to relax enough to feel my hunched shoulders drop from the back of my neck. Then, a loud rapping on the front door of the porch startled me. I jerked and spilled a few splashes of tea onto my desk. I silently cursed and got up. I came through the passageway and looked through the door's peephole. A huge blue eye stared back at me. We both jumped back from the door at the same time. "Who is it?" I asked.

"The police. Open up," came a gruff voice.

I gingerly opened the door and immediately recognized the policeman standing there. Years ago, when I'd been selling myself on the street, I'd tried to proposition him. I clearly remembered that he'd hesitated before he reluctantly turned me down. "What do you want?" I demanded.

He looked at me in surprise, and his face reddened as he remembered me. He pulled out his ID and badge to show me. Before he flipped it closed, I read his name—Samuel Miller. He held out a photo. "Do you know this man?"

My hands shook as I reached for the photo. I knew all too well who it was—the same small Asian man who'd come to my door the night before. "No, I don't," I answered honestly.

The policeman's gaze bore into mine. "Well, your neighbor seems to think you do. Said he saw you talking to him on your porch last night."

Of course, he did, I thought. My neighbor was always snooping around the neighborhood, not wanting to miss out on anything happening. "Yes, he knocked on my door, but he couldn't speak English very well, and I couldn't understand what he wanted. Sorry, but that's all I know. Why? What did he do?"

He studied me and remained silent for a few seconds. "Died," he stated flatly.

My heart thudded. "Oh, no! What happened?"

He stared at me, "Apparently, you were the last to see him alive."

"Obviously, I was NOT the last to see him alive since I certainly didn't kill him," I declared hotly.

"Sorry, ONE of the last then," he amended, slightly flustered.

"Who is he? How did he die and where was he found?"

He held his hands up in a defensive mode. "Whoa! I'm not at liberty to tell you. It's an ongoing investigation."

"How long do you think it'll take before this is all over the news or on YouTube? It doesn't make sense for you not to tell me anything since I'll find out soon enough."

"You've got a point there," he agreed. "But you're still not going to hear about it from me."

"Well then, I guess we're done here," I said and turned to go inside.

He grabbed my arm. "Not so fast, lady."

"What now?" I asked, annoyed as I felt his grip tighten.

He nodded to my sign attached to the side of the front door with an arrow indicating my office was to the side of the house. "Just what is it you do now?" he asked.

"What does that have to do with anything?" I asked as I pulled away from him.

"I just want to know," he said sincerely.

"I'm a counselor, not that it's any of your business," I replied, as I began to close the door.

His footsteps resounded as he climbed down the stairs, but not before I heard him say, "Good."

I locked the door and leaned back against it. My heart was still pounding, and it had nothing to do with the fact that Samuel Miller was an extremely handsome man. Good lord! I didn't want to be involved in any way to a murder that'd taken place. So why had that Asian man come to *me*? Who had sent him? Why?

I was vulnerable now. I had to make sure that any communication between myself and the other angels couldn't be traced. I reached for the throwaway untraceable cell phone I'd bought for such an occasion as this and called the ranch. Betsy answered.

"We've got a problem with Sue-Ling. Rather than try to explain it over the phone, I'll come out to the ranch tonight."

Betsy, always pragmatic, said, "Not to worry. Whatever it is, we'll figure it out together. Be careful, and make sure you're not followed."

CHAPTER 12

I was only too happy to see the backside of my last client of the day. I kept having to remind myself to be patient with her as she continued to complain about things from the past. Living in the past took away all joy in the present. As many times as we went over her same predicament, she was still stuck—taking on her past as her sole story and sticking to it. Maybe it was time for her to find another counselor.

I set the timer for the night light, punched in my security code to my house alarm, and left out the back door to get to my car. As I backed out of the driveway, I scanned my neighbor's house to see if he was at his lookout post. I didn't see him, and I breathed a sigh of relief. I didn't like the idea that he seemed to watch my every move. It made me uncomfortable. Even after the wear and tear of the lost years, I still turned heads with my beauty, but I no longer reveled in it. I had no desire to entice any man into having sex, for it bothered me to realize just how easy it was to do.

There was an expression I'd heard, "men were just looking for a place to put it," that removed any romance or love from the sex act for me. The other angels said this was something I'd have to work out before I could even consider having any loving, sexual relationship with a man. And to do that, they said, I'd have to forgive myself for my past choices. It was the only way I'd be able to resurrect any relationship with my parents as well. As much as I was aware that they were right, I wasn't quite there yet.

As I headed for the ranch, for the first six miles or so, I kept checking my rearview mirror to make sure that no one was following me. I even backtracked a few blocks before I headed out of the city. We were stuck with Sue-Ling whether we liked it or not, I thought unkindly. However, she was a "sister of the streets," and we needed to help her get squared away enough to move on. She was the only one who could make that a reality.

Our role was quite simple. The girls Lester and Lucy brought to us stayed with us until we were able to move them away from Nevada into rehab or a safe house, without all the cumbersome regulations and paperwork usually required. For those heavy into drugs, wherever we sent them, they'd have a chance to detox in one of the hospitals there first. An interesting thing we'd discovered was that we needed to move them on as quickly as possible so that they wouldn't get too comfortable and dependent being with us and become afraid to leave us. We were simply a stepping stone to help them get clean and sober and remain safe from their traffickers. We hoped that by each of us modeling our success when they stayed with us, they'd begin to realize they had value no matter what'd taken place and were free to live a better life—and deserved it.

Lester and Lucy's non-profit paid for all expenses at the ranch, including food for us and the animals. They also paid the costs for moving the runaway girls away from Nevada. It was their generosity that made us able to help nearly 40 girls so far, something they delighted in. Each new girl coming through the ranch was a reminder to them of what had happened to their daughter. I marveled at their willingness to continue to help girls like me and the others.

When I pulled into the ranch, it was strange to see a man outside playing ball with Sarah—Jerome. They turned and waved. I got out of my car, and Sarah was right there in my arms. "Auntie Tiff! Come play ball with us!"

"Maybe later, okay?"

She looked disappointed for a second then raced back to Jerome. "It's my turn to throw the ball."

I grinned, and Jerome winked at me before tossing the ball to Sarah.

When I entered the house, Scout lumbered forward to greet me. Lately, it was harder for him to move around, and a quick pang of sorrow shot through me when I realized he was getting old. "It's quiet in here. Where are the girls, Scout?"

He turned away and led me into the kitchen and out the back door. The girls were gathered around the hen house, staring at something crumbled on the ground. As I got closer, I could see it was one of the hens covered in blood, and it looked like the fence surrounding the hen house was partially torn down. "A hungry coyote?" I asked as I approached them. They looked up and nodded their heads.

Missy looked distraught. She hated to see anything injured, much less dead. "Dammit, he got our best laying hen!" she moaned. "Poor thing," she added as she picked up the dead hen and tenderly placed it in the garbage bag Betsy held out.

Betsy eyed me and shook her head in disgust. "I should have shot him when I had the chance."

Linda said, "Lesson learned. Here, give me the bag, and I'll dump it in the garbage."

I watched Sue-Ling as she listened to our conversation, looking from one of us to the other, not saying a word. I wondered what she thought of us—an odd foursome who'd experienced the darker side of living and had been thrown together to help someone like her. I didn't think she was very impressed with us, and I had to force myself not to laugh out loud. In her shoes, I probably wouldn't have been either.

Missy lifted the broken fence from the ground. "Sue-Ling and I will fix the fence. Meanwhile, let's get all the other hens into the hen house."

"This is another warning for us to stay close to the house. Especially in the early morning and in the later afternoon when the coyotes are searching for food. Got that, Sue-Ling?" Betsy said.

Sue-Ling nodded and stepped forward to help Missy with the fence. I waved to Betsy and Linda to follow me. We needed to discuss what'd happened since I'd left them less than 36 hours ago.

We went into the Bat Room and gathered around the large, long table where Linda worked. It was big enough that two people could comfortably work there, and Jerome's computer was open next to Linda's. He was still outside, playing with Sarah.

After I told them what happened, Betsy asked, "Do you think this was a family member? Any idea how we should handle this with Sue-Ling?"

"I think it should be more than me who meets with her."

"Probably Missy then, don't you think? Linda asked. "I think Betsy and I scare her a bit as it is."

"Speak for yourself," said Betsy with a snort. "You with your nose ring and rainbow hair."

Linda laughed. "You're just jealous because you heard Sarah say she wanted hair just like mine," she taunted in jest.

Betsy laughed and agreed. "Yes, she says she likes purple the best."

As I watched them, a wave of pleasure washed over me at seeing them tease each other. It hadn't always been that way.

"What are you doing?" Betsy asked Linda with frustration.

"Nothing," Linda answered on the defensive, as she stood straight from bending over the bassinette.

"I put her down for a nap, and no one should be in here disturbing her," scolded Betsy.

Tiffany had followed Betsy into Sarah's bedroom. Betsy's strong personality could be overbearing at times, and she was having a difficult time sharing her daughter with the rest of them. Realizing that she'd no intentions of letting the father know of his child—that is, even if she knew—made them realize just how much of a loner Betsy was. But Linda was not to be pushed around. "You need to understand something once and all. Yes, this little girl is your daughter, there's no doubt about that. But as another girl in this house, she is part of our sisterhood. We're all in this together. So get used to the idea because no one here is going to allow you to isolate Sarah away from us all her life," Linda sputtered.

Betsy stood still with her mouth hanging open. Linda had been the quiet, shy one, so for her to speak out like that was unusual. And it had its effect. Betsy looked at Tiffany for support, but she raised her shoulders as if to say, "You two work it out," and backed away, leaving them to work it out between them.

"Okay, I'll ask Missy to sit in with us. I think we'll need to see how much Sue-Ling shared with others about us because it was no small thing (no pun intended) that the little Asian man had been told to come to my place. And we don't know who else knows anything about what we do."

Linda smiled at my pun while Betsy rolled her eyes. Then both sobered up at the thought that someone might disturb what we had going on at the ranch. "Also, I spoke with Lucy and Lester, and they suggested that we lay low."

The three of us looked at each other, sizing up what the other thought. Finally, Linda spoke. "We'll still watch the perps to see what they're up to, okay?"

Betsy and I nodded in agreement. "I'm worried about what the FBI might find on Jerome's computer that might lead to us," I added.

"So is Jerome, to be honest," said Linda. Then she groaned, and we looked at her as she slapped her head. "Dammit."

"What?" Betsy and I chorused.

"Have you double-checked your phones to make sure the tracking is turned off? I need to check Sue-Ling's phone. Where is she now? Still outside with Missy?"

We marched as a unit to the window to peer outside. Missy and Sue-Ling were finishing re-attaching the fence back into place with new nails. While Linda headed outside, both Betsy and I checked our phones. We heard Sarah and Jerome come into the house, and I stepped out into the hallway. "Jerome, will you do me a favor? Can you check my car to make sure there's no tracker on it?"

"Sure. Want me to do it right now?"

"If you don't mind, that'd be great. I think there's still enough daylight to work with."

"Auntie Tiff, what's wrong with your car?"

"Nothing, I hope. How are you, little one? Did you have fun with Jerome?"

"Yes, he's a pretty good pitcher, you know."

"He is, is he? That's good!" I said as I winked at Betsy over Sarah's head.

"Come with me, Sarah. Auntie Tiff has work to do, and we'll set the table for dinner," said Betsy.

I greeted Missy and Sue-Ling as they came through the door and pulled them into the office. They both eyed me with an unspoken question as to why I'd asked them to join me. "We've had several things come up, and I need to discuss them with you both. Have a seat, you two."

Missy immediately responded, "Sure, that's fine with me."

"Sue-Ling?"

"Okay, I guess."

"You told me that you'd lived with your uncle. Is he still alive?"

Sue-Ling nodded. "Why?"

"Does he live here in Las Vegas?"

"No. He lives with my mother in Los Angeles."

"What is this all about?" interceded Missy.

"I had an older Asian man come to where I lived last night, and he asked about you, Sue-Ling. Do you know who that might have been?"

Sue-Ling blanched, and she looked at me in surprise. "What did he say?"

"He said he wanted you to come home. Was that your uncle, or is there someone else we should be worried about?"

"What did he look like?" she asked with a reddening face.

"I'd say that he was in his late 50s or early 60s. I'm not always good at guessing age."

"It was probably my uncle. I don't know who else it could be unless he was one of my clients," she mumbled.

"The problem is," I continued, "that he somehow connected me to you. I want the truth, Sue-Ling. Who have you talked to about me or being here?"

"Nobody, honest!"

I was out of patience. "I said I want the truth, Sue-Ling, so no more bull shit." I leaned forward and grabbed her arm, and twisted it around so I could check for any fresh skin pricks. "You owe me the truth."

"Hey, don't touch me, bitch!" she yelled. "I don't owe you anything!" she hollered as she yanked her arm away from me.

"What about Missy? Or Betsy and Linda? Or how about Sarah? Do you think that you don't owe them the truth so that they can be safe?"

Her eyes fluttered at the mention of Sarah. "Listen," I backed down. "Let's talk this out. Linda checked your phone, and the tracking device was off, so that's good. But for your uncle to show up on my doorstep, he had to have heard of our connection somehow. Who would know anything about what you were going to do? Think about it for a minute. Does anyone come to mind?"

Sue-Ling lifted her troubled eyes and looked directly at me. "I might have said something to Lulu, one of the girls I've gotten to know. She'd heard that there was a lady counselor in old downtown Vegas who helped girls like us, so I said that I was going to look you up."

Her words rang true. It wasn't the first time I'd heard my name passed on to a girl in trouble who was seeking help for counseling. Most of my clients were well aware of my past and were willing to talk about their own doings without the shame felt when they shared information with those who hadn't experienced what they had. As far as I knew, no one looked to me as a means of escape.

"Where can I find this, Lulu?" I asked.

"She's usually in the bar at one of the Casinos near Fremont Street on a Friday and Saturday night. Those are the only nights she works."

"What does she look like?"

Sue-Ling face broke out in a smile. "You can't miss her! Lulu's a he! Tall, black, and always wears red."

I was shocked as I observed Sue-Ling. Just by smiling, her whole face lit up, and she transformed into a real stunner. Her eyes sparkled, and there was a teasing way about her, which I could see would draw men to her. That and her petite size would bring about a masculine sense to protect her. For Sue-Ling, the one person who should have been there for her—her boyfriend—had let her down in a big way. What a crazy world we lived in today. I shook off the thought and said, "Yup. That'll make it easy to find her, alright," I laughed.

Sue-Ling bowed her head low, and the light around her closed down.

"You know, Sue-Ling, when we're angry, we all say things that we don't mean to say. At the very least, I know that's been true for me. The last time you and your boyfriend argued, did you threaten to leave him?" I watched her slowly nod her head. "If so, something might have slipped out when he asked where you'd go. Remember, guys, like your boyfriend, always think that you never have a place to go."

Tears ran down Sue-Ling's face. "He told me that no one would help me. He'd said, 'Good luck with that one, loser. If you're not here when I get back, I'll track you down and kill you. Got that?'"

"What did you do then?" I asked Sue-Ling in a soft voice.

Between hiccups, she answered, "After he went, I packed my bag and left."

I felt a wash of relief in hearing that. It now made sense. Sue-Ling'd already packed her bag, intending to leave with or without our help. But it made me wonder where she'd thought she'd be safe. "Where were you headed?"

"I had no idea. I just knew I had to get as far away from him as possible."

"So how did you end up at the soup kitchen?"

She looked at me with a sheepish look. "I was hungry."

Missy and I chuckled. "Then what?" I asked.

"Then, one of the workers there asked me a few questions, and that is when Lester talked to me."

Ahh. Now things were becoming clear. "Well, I know I speak for all of us when I say that we're glad that you're here with us. But we need to be very careful so that this place isn't discovered, and we're all safe, do you understand? We're in this together. If you think of anything that was said that can disrupt our safety, you need to let us know right away, okay?"

This time instead of being angry, Sue-Ling whispered, "Okay."

"I'm sorry to tell you this, Sue-Ling, but I'm afraid I have some very bad news for you. The man who came to my door was murdered that same night. So, if he was your uncle, the police might be trying to find you. That means that you must remain close to the house here; do you understand? We don't want anything to happen to you or to any of us."

Sue-Ling began to cry in earnest, and Missy stepped forward and held her in her arms. "And I need to ask you for your cell phone so that we can monitor it for the next few days and trace any calls that come in on it. I'm sorry, but we can't take any chances," I added, knowing this would be hard for her to do—give up the only independence left to her. I tipped my head toward the door, indicating that I'd leave them alone, and Missy nodded in agreement, and I left.

So far, it seemed we now had three people in the house wanted by either the FBI, the police, or predators – Jerome, Sue-Ling, and me.

CHAPTER 13

I left the office with a heavy heart and headed into the Bat Room to talk to Linda and Jerome. I needed to find out whether Jerome had heard any news from the FBI. I also wanted to know whether he'd found a tracker on my car.

"Hi, Jerome. Any tracker in my car?"

"Nope. You're all clear. I'll check your car each time you're here. I think it'd be a good idea for me to show all of you the main places trackers are placed on a car so you can check for yourselves."

"That's a good idea. Linda, did you tell Jerome what Lester said about laying low for a bit?"

"We've agreed that we'd still be able to interrupt the broadcasting of any advertising of the auction or the actual auction itself. That'd make it impossible for the viewers to see the girls. Then, when the perps are trying to clear up the reception, it might give us enough time to locate where they're filming. Then, we can report their location to the special task force, and we've got 'em!"

"And that's safe to do?" I asked.

"As long as our code can outsmart their code," responded Jerome.

After Jerome had shown all of us the usual locations in my car where trackers are found, we were somber as we returned to the house. Missy took out the casserole she had heated up in the oven, and, except for Sarah, we sat at the table subdued while we ate our dinner. Sarah chatted on about playing ball with Jerome, and we smiled, even though our minds were elsewhere, filled with worry. Looking around the table, I thought how awful it'd be if anything broke up this usually happy family. I sighed and rose from the table to clear the dishes. It was my turn to clean up, and I was glad for the distraction.

Shortly after I'd finished, I headed upstairs to my room. I'd get up early and head back to the city. The girls and I thought it best for me to keep to the schedule I'd had before unless something untold happened. I'd return Friday when it was customary for me to do so.

While waiting for my first client the next day, I scanned the newspaper I'd picked up to see whether there was an article about my visitor who had been murdered. Nothing. I looked at the classified ads to see whether anything stuck out regarding an unusual ad, which could mean an inference to the upcoming sex auction. Again, nothing.

I felt terrible for the policemen because it was so challenging to keep up with all that happened in Las Vegas. There are 5 to 6 people who go missing each day—over 200 each month. Of all murders committed, only 60% of them ever got solved, and that statistic held nationwide. It was still early for my client when I heard someone pounding on my front door. I tensed with alarm but forced myself to walk forward to see who it was. This time, I didn't bother with the peephole and opened the main door, leaving the safety screen locked. My heart fell when I saw who it was—Samuel Miller, the same policeman who'd been there before.

"What do you want, officer?" I asked.

"We need you to come down to the police station."

"Why? I haven't done anything."

"We need to question you regarding the Asian man you were talking to the other night."

"I've told you all I know. I've nothing more to say," I said in a dismissive tone.

"We've new evidence, and we need you down at the station," he insisted.

"I have a client arriving here in a few minutes." I sighed in exasperation. "Can I meet you at the station later?"

"How long is your appointment?" he asked, looking at his watch.

"One hour," I answered.

"Okay. I'll be back in exactly one hour, and you'd better be ready to go." He looked over his shoulder as my client drove up and parked. He left, mumbling, "One hour."

Since most of my clients aren't too keen on the police, I smiled at my client and said, "No worries. The police are collecting money for one of their charities."

I let her into the house, and we maneuvered into the office from inside the main house. "Would you like a cup of coffee?" I asked.

We sipped our coffee and took the full hour to discuss her problem. After the timer went off, signaling one hour had passed, I rose and walked my client to her car. Thankfully, Samuel didn't pull up in his cruiser until after she'd gone. "Wait, I'll get my purse and lock up," I called to him.

He got out of his car and stood by its side and waited for me. When I returned, he opened the back door and let me climb in without pushing my head down as I remembered from the past. Knowing I was locked inside made me shiver, and my stomach turned. This ride brought back bad times and one specific lousy memory.

"I didn't do anything wrong!" she squealed.

"Nothing wrong? You think selling yourself on the street is right? A beautiful woman like you? You're selling yourself short is what you're doing!" he yelled at her.

She looked at him, taking him in. "I'll give you the best blow job you've ever had," she urged, "if you let me go."

She was so high she nearly missed his mumbled words, "I bet you could." Then, he stood and stared at her. Angrily, he grabbed her arm and pulled her to the cruiser, forcing her into the back. He swore, "Goddammit, woman. Get in the car now!"

She felt his anger was different—not directed at her, but at something beyond them both. She swore she'd never forget his face, and she hadn't.

Right now, here she was staring at that same face by way of the rearview mirror. I shivered again and leaned forward. "What's happened for you to bring me in?"

"We'll talk about it at the station."

I leaned back, unhappy with his answer. I hadn't contacted the girls to let them know what was going on, especially since there was little they could do at this point.

When we got to the station, Samuel came around and held the door open for me to get out. As I swung my bare legs onto the ground, I caught him staring at them, and he blushed. I ignored him, and he took hold of my arm as if I were an old lady and led me forward. When we walked through the door, heads turned our way.

"Down here," he said with his hand on the small of my back, pushing me forward. "Stop right here," he demanded and gently guided me into the bare room with just a table and two chairs that sat across from each other.

"Whatever you've come up with must be something awful for you to treat me like a criminal," I said, and Samuel's face reddened.

"Have a seat, and I'll be back in a minute," he said.

Several long minutes later, Samuel and a female cop came into the room, dragging another chair. I assumed she must be his partner even though they neither confirmed nor denied it. "Hi, Tiffany. My name is Officer Shirley McKnight, and both Officer Miller and I have some questions for you. I believe Officer Miller told you we have new evidence that puts you in a negative light regarding the murder of Mr. Ling. Why don't you tell us exactly what happened that night?"

"What is the new evidence?"

"First, why don't you tell us what happened that night."

"Exactly what I told Officer Miller," I stated with a pounding heart. "He came to the door and spoke to me, but I couldn't make out what he said or what he wanted. After a few minutes, he left. End of story."

"Can you tell me why he'd have your name and address jotted down on a note inside his jacket?"

Luckily, I had no warning beforehand of this, so my surprise was genuine, which they noticed. "I have no idea. I'm a counselor, and perhaps he was looking to make an appointment. Who knows?"

"Did he say this in his conversation with you?" asked Samuel.

I shook my head. "Not that I could make out."

"Maybe he was looking for information about one of your clients," suggested Samuel.

"Could be. I just don't know."

"Who are your typical clients?" asked Shirley.

"Most of them are overcoming addictions. I can't say more than that without it being against client privilege."

Shirley gave Samuel a small nod and said, "Fair enough. You're free to go for now, but don't leave the area, understood?"

"I'll drive you back home," Samuel said. I caught a look that passed between him and Shirley. He headed to the door and stood there, waiting for me to pass through it.

When we reached the car outside, he put his hand on my shoulder and turned to me. "Tiffany, here's my card. If you're ever in trouble, please feel free to call me." I looked up at him in surprise. "I mean it. You can trust me," he stated sincerely.

The unspoken look in his eyes made me blush, and I felt a twinge of something I'd put aside years before. I glanced at his card, and it read that he was a detective, something I hadn't noticed before. "Why would you want to help me?"

"Let's just say that I have a vested interest in keeping you safe."

"And just what would that vested interest be?" I challenged.

His cell phone rang, and it was easy to read the relief on his face as he ignored my question and answered the phone. As he was talking, he opened the back door of the cruiser and guided me inside. Then he walked around to the driver's seat and hopped in.

When he pulled up to the curb in front of my house, Samuel released the locked door. I hurriedly got out and practically ran up the sidewalk. I got inside before he was barely out of the cruiser. He stood by the car, looking puzzled before he took off.

I didn't want to waste any time dwelling about what Samuel had said; yet, I surprised myself by putting his information into my cell phone before tossing out the card he had given me.

I had things to do. Instead of driving to the ranch on Friday, I'd pop into the bar at the Casino off Fremont Street, where I thought Lulu would be hanging out. According to Sue-Ling's description, she shouldn't be hard to find.

CHAPTER 14

The week flew by, and I remained at home, laying low without attracting attention. I'd spoken with the girls several times via my private cell phone, and all seemed well at the ranch. Sue-Ling was having a tough go of it, but that was to be expected. I felt sorry for her and all she was going through. Human trafficking and all it entailed was such an awful thing with long-lasting effects, especially dealing with the idea that the victim has no power. And the number of runaways that went into the streets prostituting themselves to survive was growing day by day as more kids were escaping abuse at home. Many of those same kids were now my clients. It was difficult for them to understand how things had gotten so far away from their dreams. Most couldn't even remember what those were anymore.

And the pain of it all brought on the drugs and their quest to escape their way of living.

On Friday night, I put on a simple slip dress and headed down to the elite bar at the Casino, hoping to meet up with Lulu. As I stepped through the doorway into the bar area, visions of the past overcame me, and I wobbled to the nearest table and sat down.

"Hey, beautiful! Can I buy you a drink?

"Sure," she replied in a daze. "Why not?"

"What's a pretty girl like you doing here?"

"Looking for you, handsome. What d'ya think?"

"Now, that's what I like to hear. What are you drinking, doll?"

"Martini straight up," she answered, scanning his body looking for signs of wealth.

"My kind of girl. If you're going to drink, drink. None of those sissy drinks for you, right, honey?"

"Sure thing."

Several drinks later, he leaned toward her. "I've got something I'd like to show you. I think you're going to like it. Most girls do. What do you say?" he asked with a wink.

She strategically placed her hand near his crotch and watched him flinch with anticipation. At this stage, she knew if she played along, she could ask for more money.

The memory of what it'd been like to play the game of street whore made me feel sick to my stomach. I started to get up to leave. As I rose, I caught Lulu's eye, staring at me from across the room. I chuckled to myself, for she was a sight to behold. She stood tall and majestic and commanded attention with her flamboyant red dress that molded her body. She was stunning with gorgeous locks of black hair that flowed around her smiling face and flashing dark eyes. Bright red lips surrounded even white teeth. Anyone would have to be dumb, deaf, and blind not to notice her. I was surprised to see her head my way, and I sucked in my breath as I watched her come closer.

"Well, well. Who have we got here?" Lulu asked in a beautiful contralto voice. "May I join you?"

"Of course. I've been hoping I'd run into you …"

Hearing those words, he straightened in his chair. "I know who you are, honey."

"You do?" I asked in astonishment.

"Yes, you're Tiffany Darling, and you helped out one of my girlfriends in a jam."

"I did?"

"Word gets around."

"Oh, I'm surprised, is all."

"Once a girl on the street, you're always part of the street." At the expression on my face, she amended, "All meant in a good way."

I nodded. "Lulu, I need to ask you. Have you recommended me to anyone recently?"

Her face became serious. "Is this about Minnie Mouse?"

"Who?"

She chuckled. "I used to call Sue-Ling Minnie Mouse because she's so little and was always so frightened—like a little mouse. But don't get fooled, she can be a beast."

"What do you mean?"

"Minnie Mouse is very clever, that's all I'll say."

"Did you recommend me to her family?"

Lulu looked me straight in the eye. "Is this about her uncle?"

"Yes, it is," I said, grateful that what Sue-Ling had said was correct.

"I wrote down your name and address for him. I thought you might know where to find her, that's all."

"Are you aware that he was murdered?"

All the blood drained from her face. "Fuck. You've got to be kidding."

"They found the note in his pocket. The police have already questioned me about it. I said nothing about where I thought the note might have come from, and I won't," I consoled as I held onto Lulu's hand.

Worry spread across her face. She looked at me with wet eyes. "I'm so sorry to get you involved."

"You were only trying to help Sue-Ling out. You have to promise me, though, that if you hear anything about the uncle or Sue-Ling, you'll call the number I'm going to give you, okay? Just leave a voice mail message. After I pick up your message, I'll delete it so it won't be able to be traced back to you."

She nodded. "Okay, girlfriend, I'll do it."

Here's my number," I said and repeated it until she had it plugged into her phone.

Lulu looked around. "I'd offer to buy you a drink, but it's getting pretty crowded in here, and I don't think it's a good idea to be seen together if you know what I mean."

Unfortunately, I knew precisely what Lulu meant. It was essential to make her moves now before the other girls stepped in, and she was left with prospects who had less money to spend on sex. She rose from her seat at the same time I did. She air-kissed me and strolled to the bar where two men were eying her lasciviously. I left the bar area as shivers crawled along my body. I couldn't get out of there fast enough.

When I got home, I tore off my clothes and jumped back into the jeans and tee-shirt I'd worn earlier and gathered my things to head out to the ranch. I readied the house for my departure and went out the back door to get into my car. As I pulled out into the street, I looked to see if any vehicle or person looked out of place. Seeing nothing unusual, I began weaving my way along the back roads to the ranch.

I arrived later than usual, and all but Linda and Jerome were in bed. They were like two night hawks focused over their computers with heads almost touching. I left them to grab a soda from the kitchen. Frick and Frack came to greet me, and I immediately went to them to cut off any barking. Their wire cage was close by, where they chose to doze together each night without anyone forcing them to sleep there. Soon Scout wandered out to see me, and I led him upstairs where he was allowed to sleep at the foot of my bed. With bad memories of my former life taunting me, I needed him near me that night.

CHAPTER 15

I woke up the next morning with Scout making mewling sounds, and his wet nose pressed against my cheek. "What's the matter, Scout?"

He hurried to the deck knocking aside the half-opened sliding door, and stood there overseeing the property. He barked, growled, and barked again. I stood behind him with my hands shielding my eyes. Although it was early, there was enough light to make out the barn and other buildings on the ranch. I reached down and patted Scout's head. "What do you see, Scout?"

He tipped his head and stared into my eyes, expecting that I'd know what he was trying to say. Unfortunately, I didn't. "Is it the coyote?" His tail began to wag furiously. Just then, I noticed movement below me and saw Betsy sneak out the back door with her shotgun. She was a light sleeper, especially after the birth of Sarah, and she must have sensed me because she looked up and put her finger across her lips. I nodded and grabbed onto Scout's collar and pulled him back into the room with me.

Although I didn't like the idea of a coyote skulking around the ranch, I liked it even less if Betsy was lucky enough to get him this time. I hated to see anything die, even understanding that was how nature worked with its pecking order. Scout was heading toward the stairs, and I called him back. "Here, boy. Stay with me. We don't want you to get in the way."

He hesitated a moment and then slowly made his way back, jumping up and plopping on the bed with a resigned sigh. I curled up beside him and nuzzled his neck. "I love you, old man," I said as I began to stroke his body. "What are we going to do with Sue-Ling, huh? She's hard for me to read, and I don't know what's she's thinking. Can I trust her, Scout?"

His pink tongue rolled across my face, and I groaned and laughed as I wiped his slurp away. "Aw right, I think before you give me a complete bath, it's time for me to get up." I grabbed my robe and headed downstairs to start the coffee. Scout was close behind, nudging me forward.

Sarah strolled into the kitchen, stretching and yawning. "Where's Mommy?"

"Outside, trying to get the coyote. Want some hot chocolate, sweetie?"

"Yes, Auntie Tiff. That'd be nice," she replied in a grownup voice before heading to the table to sit down. Then she changed her mind and went to the cupboard and reached for the box of cereal. "I want some cereal too."

"Okay, sit down, and I'll get everything set, okay?"

"Yup. Is Jerome going to stay here forever, Auntie Tiff?"

"I don't think so. Why?"

"I like him being here."

"Well, we'll have to wait and see what happens, won't we?"

"Yup," she said as she picked up her hot chocolate to sip.

The back door banged open, making both Sarah and me jump. "Damn that coyote! He's too clever for me, the bastard. He got away this time, but at least he didn't get one of our hens," grumbled Betsy. She paused when she noticed Sarah at the table. "Good morning, sweetheart. I didn't see you there."

"I know, and you said a bad word."

Betsy and I looked at each other and tried not to laugh. "That's right, I did. I'm sorry."

Sarah nodded. "That's okay."

"How about a cup of coffee?" I asked Betsy.

"Sounds good."

Missy came in wearing her bathrobe instead of being dressed for the day as she usually did. Her hair was standing on end, and she looked like she'd had a rough night. "I couldn't sleep."

"That's easy to see. Here, have a seat, and I'll pour you a cup of coffee," I offered.

"Did you check in on Sue-Ling before you came down?" Betsy asked.

"Yes, she's still asleep. It's too early. She usually gets up later."

"How's she doing, Missy?"

"To tell the truth, I'm worried about her. She's still very upset about her uncle's death, and now she's worried about her mother. Betsy and I let her call her mother using one of our special phones, and I don't know if her mother fully understands what has happened. But Sue-Ling isn't safe going to see her mother—not when her boyfriend is probably still looking for her."

"Does she have any idea who might have wanted to kill her uncle?"

"She's been very quiet. She hasn't said much about anything. But when I asked her if it could have been her boyfriend, her face got all red, and she turned away from me. That might be something to look into, don't you think?"

Betsy and I nodded. Samuel Miller's face flashed across my mind. Would he be able to help us? I let that thought go and replaced it with Lulu being the one to give us more information.

Betsy and I worked together to make breakfast. The smell of coffee and bacon cooking first drew out Linda, Jerome, and then Sue-Ling, who hesitated in the doorway before joining us. We sat around the table, and it was quiet until Sarah asked, "Jerome, are you going to live here forever?"

Her question caught him off guard, and he sputtered out coffee. We chuckled as he grabbed a napkin and wiped his mouth before cleaning up the spatters of coffee. "No, Sarah, I'm not. I'm just visiting for a few weeks."

He blushed and looked at Linda with a hidden smile, and I immediately wondered what was going on between them. I'd have thought Linda would be the last of us ever to be interested in a relationship with a man. When I first met her, I thought she was gay with her short hair, tattoos, and rough manner. Eying her now, I found it hard to believe I'd thought that. Her cheeks were pink, and her eyes sparkled as she gave Jerome a wide smile. Then, she lightly punched his arm. "We'll have to see about that, won't we?"

I turned away and noticed Sue-Ling's gaze fixated on Linda. She had spent the least amount of time with Linda, and I wondered what Sue-Ling thought about Linda and Jerome's comfortable relationship. I doubted her relationship with her boyfriend had been anything close to that. "Sue-Ling, if you have a few minutes, let's meet after breakfast. Maybe you could join us, Missy?"

"Sure," Missy responded, but Sue-Ling didn't say anything. No matter, because it was time to get more information about her boyfriend. Was he someone who'd track Sue-Ling down no matter what and put us all in jeopardy?

CHAPTER 16

After Sue-Ling and Missy were seated, I closed the door, and instead of sitting behind the desk, I sat on the love seat across from them to make our meeting more casual.

"Sue-Ling, we need to know more about your boyfriend. What's his full name?"

"Johnny Wong," she answered reluctantly.

"How long has he been here in Las Vegas? Did you come with him?"

"Yes, we came here three years ago."

"I'm curious to know if he immediately started you out on the street."

"No, he wanted me all to himself," she stated proudly. "It wasn't until later when he met some friends that I began doing tricks."

"How serious is he about hunting you down? Is he the type that won't quit until he finds you?"

"I'm sure he still wants me with him," she stated.

My heart fell. Sue-Ling wasn't ready to give him up. "Can you please explain what you mean by his wanting you with him?"

"I know he still loves me ..." she trailed off. With a challenging look, she dared me to refute what she'd said.

"So, what do you plan to do, Sue-Ling? Go back to Johnny and let him beat you up anytime he wants?"

"Noo," she answered defensively.

"And what about the drugs? Do you want to keep pumping them into your body until the day you don't wake up and are found lying in an alley somewhere?"

"Noo," she whispered, fear in her eyes.

"Well, you get to choose. It's up to you, you know."

Sue-Ling looked down at the floor.

"So, here's the deal. You're going to have to help us decide what to do with you. You might be interested to know that so far, each woman who has come through here *wanted* to escape her pimp and stop selling herself on the streets—*and* she wanted to be drug-free. And guess what? Each one of them has succeeded!"

Sue-Ling looked up at my enthusiastic announcement and waited to see what I'd say next.

"But to be honest, I don't see that you're serious about wanting the same thing—what they craved. And to stay here, you need to convince us otherwise. Do you understand?"

Sue-Ling flashed a look at Missy for confirmation, who nodded in agreement. "You have to be ready to do what is necessary to get clean and sober. And you must want more than anything to leave the streets, or it won't work."

"What will happen to me if I can't do it?"

"We'll cross that bridge when it happens. Again, Sue-Ling, being here at the ranch, is only a stepping stone. While you wait for a vacancy at a rehab house, we're here to acclimate you to being away from the streets and your pimp."

"Where will I go?"

"To a good place far from here." As a look of fear flashed across her face, I added, "You'll never be alone either. You'll always have someone with you to protect you."

I couldn't tell whether she was relieved or upset to learn that. I looked at Missy to question whether we were finished. She nodded and rose from her chair, reaching for Sue-Ling. "Let's get dressed and start our chores."

"Okay, you two. I'm going to get dressed too and exercise Big Red," I said, with that happy thought.

CHAPTER 17

As I threw my leg over Big Red, I felt a sense of peace wash over me. Scout was standing by, refusing to be left behind. I thought it would be good exercise for him, and I vowed to keep our pace fairly slow. Missy held the gate open for us, and we headed up to the ridge along the mountains, which held a magnificent view of our small valley below. It amazed me that so many people, thinking they had gotten lost on a dead-end road, didn't travel far enough down the road to discover the ranch. That allowed us enough privacy to make us believe that we were all alone for miles and miles. But the truth was that just a few miles to the west of us was another fairly large ranch that used to belong to the sibling of the original owner of our ranch. Every once in a while, while riding Big Red, I'd bump into that owner. He'd always tease me about Big Red riding Big Red, a poor joke that made him laugh and laugh.

"Let's try to get to the top of the ridge, Big Red. What d'ya think?"

Big Red snorted and drew her head up and down, pulling at the reins. "Okay, then, let's get going!" I yelled. We raced across the field and headed for the ridge. "Hee-haw!" I hollered, and Big Red picked up her pace. Scout stayed with us, huffing and puffing with a big doggy grin. My heart leaped with joy.

Finally, when we reached the ridge, I pulled in Big Red, and we trotted to a grassy area that was cooled by the towering pine trees growing there. I swung myself down and threw the reins over Big Red's head, giving her the freedom to move around and nibble the grass. I grabbed the knapsack from behind the saddle and removed a treat for Scout and poured water for him into a small bowl. Then, I gave Big Red an apple to munch on while I sipped fresh coffee from a thermos.

As I sat there, I studied the valley below and made out a figure walking through the brush from my neighbor's direction. It looked as if he were carrying a shotgun. I was transfixed watching him; he seemed unaware we were above him. I rose and got out the binoculars that I always carried with me in my knapsack. I was startled when I zoomed in on the figure and saw he was Asian. I immediately took out my cell phone and called Betsy. "We've got a visitor, Betsy, and it doesn't look good. You all better clear out now and go into hiding. I'm on the ridge, and I'll ride down to intercept him."

"Who is it?"

"I think it's Sue-Ling's boyfriend, but I'm not sure."

"Let me know as soon as you can, okay?"

"For sure. Gotta go."

We made our way down there at full gallop and startled the man as we rode toward him at full speed. He looked away as if looking for an escape route. I pulled back on Big Red at the very last minute, making it impossible not to miss the fear in his eyes. "This is private property. What are you doing here?" I demanded.

"Looking for the coyote. He got one of our hens this morning. He's got to be around here somewhere."

"What do you mean, 'he got one of our hens'? Do you work at the Meadows Ranch?"

He grinned. "Kinda, unless I can get away with it."

"What does that mean?"

"My father owns Meadows Ranch; I'm his adopted son, Richard. You can call me Rick, though. And you are?"

"Tiffany Darling," I replied, hating the sound of my name.

"Ahh. You're the fearless Big Red my father talks about."

I blushed and ignored his remark. "You won't find the coyote at this time of day. He usually doesn't come out until dusk and early morning. He's probably hiding up in the mountain."

He stood there, baffled. "Oh, well then, I guess I'd better head back home."

I nodded in agreement. "Say hello to your father for me, will you?"

"Sure," he smiled. "He'll be sorry to miss you."

I was surprised by Rick's comment, but I didn't respond. I mounted Big Red, and Scout rose from where he'd plopped down, and we cantered back to the ranch. I called Betsy as I rode. "All clear. I'll explain when I get back."

As we pulled into the paddock, all of the others were standing there waiting to hear what'd happened. "I didn't realize our neighbor had an adopted son. Did any of you?"

They all shook their heads. "Anyway, when I looked through the binoculars, I saw a young man who looked like it could have been Sue-Ling's boyfriend carrying a shotgun. He was looking for the coyote who'd gotten one of their hens this morning."

"That's it, then?" asked Linda.

"Yeah, but it's made me think that anyone looking for Sue-Ling wouldn't necessarily come marching down our road to the ranch. They could hold up on the mountain and pounce when they wanted, coming in from the back."

"You're right," confirmed Betsy.

"Why don't we set up an alarm system out here as well as inside the house?" suggested Jerome.

"That's a great idea," Missy and Linda said together.

"Order what you need and have it sent to my house, and I'll bring it out the next time I come," I suggested.

"Sounds like a plan," said Jerome before heading back to the house.

Betsy stayed back with me while the others went their various ways, and I led Big Red into the barn. "I don't like this one bit, Tiff. Something doesn't feel right about this whole situation."

"I agree," I said as I pulled the saddle from Big Red's back and began to rub him down. "I don't like that there's a murder connected to me somehow. What do you think we should do?"

"I think we should get Sue-Ling moved along as soon as possible. I've checked with our sources, and no one has a bed open for her yet. So we're probably looking at one week at least. Missy has Sue-Ling on the meds that'll help her until a bed becomes available." She shook her head. "I don't understand why Lester took this one in."

"Me, neither, but it is what it is, right?"

"Yeah, we can't cry over spilled milk, for sure. Too late for that."

CHAPTER 18

After Betsy left, I brushed Big Red until his coat gleamed while all the time, my mind raced. I needed to contact Lulu to see if she'd heard anything more about Sue-Ling being missing, her uncle's death, or even any street news about Sue-Ling's boyfriend and pimp. I felt something was brewing, and Sue-Ling knew more than she was admitting.

Walking back to the house, I heard Sarah's laughter coming from the front. When I got closer, I peeked around the corner to see Jerome playing ball with her. I stood there unobserved and watched the two of them. Jerome seemed to be such a nice guy, and I wondered what would happen to him if the FBI discovered what we'd done and his part in it. The FBI didn't always play nice, and his helping us could destroy him in many ways. Although I had a feeling that between Linda and him, they'd been able to cover their tracks, worry wouldn't leave me.

I slipped away and went into the house. Missy and Sue-Ling were in the kitchen fixing sandwiches for lunch. "After lunch, Sue-Ling, we'll have our regular session, then we'll be done for the day. I'm thinking of going back to town afterward."

"Really?" Missy asked, surprised.

"Yeah, I've got a few things I want to catch up on."

"Do the others know?"

"I'll tell them at lunchtime."

I'd made my decision on the spur of the moment. I needed to talk to Lulu. The best time to do that was going to be tonight, back at the casino's bar. I hated the thought of going down there again, but I'd do whatever I needed to do.

Sue-Ling asked if Missy could join us for the meeting. She looked at Missy as her protector, and I had no problem with that. I'd had time to think about the approach I wanted to use with Sue-Ling, and as I remembered back to what had helped me when I'd first joined Lester and Lucy, I decided to follow their advice.

> At Lester's suggestion that she find something to aim for, to work toward, and that'd keep her mind off craving a drink or a sniff of coke, she'd responded, "I don't know what it is you want me to do."
>
> "All I want you to do is think about something that'd make you happy, something you'd look forward to, and you'd be pleased to achieve. Have you thought about

what that could be?"

"No ..."

"It can be anything, Tiffany. Once you set your mind to it, I know you can accomplish it. You've got what it takes; you must know that."

"But I don't know what it is!" she squealed in frustration.

"Tiffany, take your time and see if anything comes to mind. Let your mind wander. Dream your dreams and see which of them makes you feel happy. Then you'll know. We'll talk about it in a few days, okay?"

She remained quiet. She didn't have the heart to tell Lester she had no dreams—they'd died a long time ago.

She was unaware that by saying what he had, Lester had stirred her soul to believe in something more. Later, when he'd suggested she become a counselor, it had awakened a yearning inside her to be more than she was.

Thinking of that time, I knew Sue-Ling probably wouldn't understand why I was prodding her to think of her future beyond the day-to-day struggle with addiction. I was hoping it'd help her begin to think there was more to her life than what she was living.

"So Sue-Ling, during this time, we've found that it's a good thing to think of what you'd like to do to keep your mind busy. If you could do anything in life, anything at all, what would it be?"

"You've got to be fucking kidding me, right?" she questioned in disgust.

"Believe me; I'm not. Think about it. What would it be? We all have to fill our days doing something. Why not do something you've always wanted to do?"

"I want to be Jennifer Lopez and make millions of dollars," she laughed bitterly.

I laughed. "Ahh. Here's the catch, Sue-Ling. You can't be someone else. This lifetime you're stuck with being you. And when you think about it, that's not so bad, is it?"

Sue-Ling remained lost in thought.

"We'll talk about it the next time I'm here. Meantime, how are you feeling?

Sue-Ling shrugged her shoulders.

"Are the meds working okay, Missy?"

"She's on the regular dose and will be until she's settled somewhere else. The medicine is helping you, isn't it, Sue-Ling?"

She nodded reluctantly in response.

I abruptly switched the topic of conversation. "If it'd turned out that our neighbor had been your boyfriend coming here, what do you think would've happened?"

Sue-Ling's head jerked my way, fear in her eyes.

"Would you have gone with him if you'd had the chance?"

Sue-Ling bowed her head.

"We need to be crystal clear about the reality of things. We can't fool ourselves that things are something other than they are. So again, I ask you, what do you think will happen if your boyfriend finds you here?"

She shrugged her shoulders.

"Do you think he'll rush into your arms and beg you to forgive him? And even if he did, would that mean he'd stop hurting you and selling you on the street?" I taunted, hoping to get a rise out of her.

She shook her head and looked up with tears rolling down her face. "NO!" she shouted. "No, he wouldn't stop! There! Does that make you happy?"

"It makes me sad," I replied. I drew in a deep breath. "Do you know of any reason why your uncle was murdered? Could he have been killed by your boyfriend, maybe because he was unsuccessful in finding you?" The question hung in the air. It was the same question that'd been haunting me. I wanted to know if it made sense to her; if so, she must be blaming herself.

As the possible truth of my words sunk in, all three of us looked at each other. The reality of what that meant was we were dealing with a killer for sure.

CHAPTER 19

I drove into town with a heavy heart. I had the awful thought that what Sue-Ling had been hiding from us was that her boyfriend had killed before, and she knew about it first-hand. Tonight, it'd be interesting to see how much Lulu knew about her boyfriend.

Later, I took my time getting dressed for the evening. My goal was to dress provocatively enough that I might attract enough attention to be approached by one of the pimps that worked the casinos – maybe even Sue-Ling's boyfriend. I didn't want the girls to know I was doing this because I was sure they would disagree with me stirring up trouble. I knew it could be dangerous, and I'd have to make sure that I was never alone.

Instead of driving myself to the casino, I called Uber for a ride, thinking that'd be the safest way to get there. After being dropped off, I felt all eyes on me as I strutted through the casino and headed to the fancy bar. I made quite an entrance and drew the attention of all who were there. Sitting at the bar, Lulu was one of the ones who looked my way. Then, she sashayed her way to where I stood, and when she got closer, she grabbed my hand, pulled it high over my head, and moved it in such a way that I had no choice but to twirl around. Her eyes shone her approval. "My, oh my! Look what you've done to yourself. You're positively gorgeous!"

I blushed and immediately halted, hating the extra stir we were making. "Lulu, can you sit with me a minute?"

"Why, girl, I'd be delighted. Are you buying? If so, I'll have a martini straight up."

I chuckled. Lulu sure knew how to work it. "Why not?" I answered and signaled for the waitress as we sat down at a small table in the corner.

Once seated, Lulu looked at me with a serious expression. "What are you up to, girl? It isn't like you to be here strutting your stuff like you are, so tell me, what's going on?"

"Can I trust you?"

"If you can't trust me, you can't trust nobody. We girls have to stick together. What happens on the street, stays on the street between us girls, understand?" She reached across the table and held my hand. "What's going on, boo? Is this about Sue-Ling?"

I nodded.

"Do you know where she is?" she asked with a worried expression.

"I might." I took a deep breath. "What can you tell me about her boyfriend? He's a bad egg, isn't he?"

"Hell, yeah. A bad egg don't describe Johnny Wong enough. Don't mess with him; he's trouble for sure."

My heart fell. "Have you heard anything about who murdered Sue-Ling's uncle?"

She leaned closer and whispered, "The word is that it was Sue-Ling's boyfriend who done him in."

My stomach somersaulted. That meant Johnny Wong probably knew where I lived. Stepping out and dressing as I'd done had not been a smart thing to do then. It would've been better for me to keep a low profile. The waitress came to the table with our drinks, followed by a man smiling broadly. "Hi ladies, can I buy these drinks for you?"

"Sure, big fella, have a seat," Lulu answered. She waited for the man to sit down and make himself comfortable before she pointedly looked at me. "Sorry, you have to be on your way. We'll be in touch real soon."

The man looked disappointed I was leaving until he watched Lulu pull at her top, revealing more of her breasts. Now more interested in what Lulu had to offer, he barely said goodbye to me. I stepped away from the table and called Uber. I made my way back through the casino, anxious to escape. When I reached the outside door, my arm was grabbed and jerked back. I was ready to deliver a chop across the perpetrator's wrist when I looked up to meet the blue eyes of Samuel Miller, the detective. "What the hell are you doing here?" he whispered. "And dressed like that?"

"What is it to you?" I snapped.

He looked surprised at my quick anger. He was out of uniform and looked more like a tourist wearing a Hawaiian shirt and shorts. I wondered what he was doing there. His legs were solid and muscled as were his arms, and he was handsome despite his angry scowl. "This isn't the place for you. Do you have a way to get home?" he asked in a gruff tone.

Just then, the Uber car pulled up, and I hopped into it without saying a word. He stood on the curb, wearing a funny expression as he watched me leave. When I got home, I cautiously walked around the house before I went in. If someone was inside, I didn't want to be trapped there. Everything looked calm and peaceful, so I punched in the alarm code and entered. Once inside, I immediately undressed and washed off the heavy makeup I'd worn. I began to shake at realizing how stupid I'd acted. What had I been thinking?

I turned on the television, and there was a news flash announcing another murder had been committed. The search was on for Blackie, a well-known pimp in the area. I shuttered when I saw his face because I'd had a run-in with him years ago when I was out on the streets. I thought he'd left Las Vegas and had moved on to another city.

Las Vegas was a fascinating city because, in reality, it was much more like a small town where everyone knew what everyone else was doing. I was worried now that by going to Lulu's chosen casino, it might have drawn enough attention to get back to some of the pimps for them to think I was doing tricks on my own. That wouldn't be good at all.

I tossed and turned most of the night, only to wake up with a headache. With the idea of buying one of their freshly made fruit and vegetable smoothies, I drove to the nearest market. As I stood in line to pay for it, I saw through the window, several people gathered around my car. My heart raced as I came forward and asked, "What's going on?"

The crowd opened, allowing me to see the words written in red across my windshield, "You die next, bitch!"

I stood there mortified, not able to say a word. I felt faint and faltered. A man stepped forward and clasped my shoulder. "I've already called the police. You better sit down over there," he said, pointing to one of the little café tables arranged outside the store.

All eyes were on me as I stumbled my way there. Who could have done this, and why? And the police had been called? A car drove in, and we all turned as an unmarked police cruiser rolled into the parking lot without its sirens blasting, and pulled alongside my car. The man, who'd urged me to sit down, walked forward to the car, leaned down, and spoke through the window to the person inside. When the door opened, and Samuel Miller stepped out, my heart fell. I was embarrassed to see him again so soon after last night. The man then led him to where I sat, and it was difficult for me to meet the detective's eyes.

"We meet again," he said with a sigh.

"It seems we do, Detective Miller."

"Sam's the name; just call me Sam." He studied me. "So, any idea why someone would do this?"

I shook my head. "No idea at all."

Another cruiser pulled in. This time it was the same policewoman who'd questioned me at the station who got out of the car. She and her partner pushed the crowd back and ordered them to disperse. She then reached inside her cruiser for a camera and took photos from several different angles. Watching her, I secretly searched the crowd looking for the possible culprit of the warning, but I saw no one who looked suspicious.

"You'll need to come down to the station to fill out a report. Do you need a ride?" When Sam saw me hesitate, he added, "You'll need to fill out a report; it helps to document provocation. We need to talk, anyhow."

"About what?" I retorted.

"Here, give me your keys, and I'll have your car driven to the station. We'll clean off the window after we take some fingerprints and samples of the paint he used. You can ride with me."

Instead of arguing with him, I handed him my keys, and he walked to the other cruiser and gave them to the policewoman. I made my way to Sam's car and opened the front passenger door and got in. I had no intention of sitting in the back seat again.

The station was not that far away, so there wasn't much time to talk, which suited me just fine. I was uncomfortable around Sam. I had the feeling that he disapproved of me even though he seemed overly protective of me at times. What was that about? So far, I hadn't been able to figure out what his game was.

Sam cleared his throat, and his cheeks redden. "About the other night, I apologize. I shouldn't have yelled at you like that. It's just that I was working undercover, and you could have gotten hurt."

"So, what's going on down there?"

"I can't talk about it. However, what I can tell you is that simply by having that Asian man visit you on the night of his murder, it connects you to his case, whether you're innocent or not. And now this—the death threat. What's going on? What are you hiding from me?"

"Nothing, honest!" What could I say without divulging the fact that we had Sue-Ling with us at the ranch? There was no way I was willing to expose the farm and let the police know what we were doing there. Some things were better left unsaid.

"I know that you don't trust me or any police for that matter. However, let me warn you that you're getting mixed up in things that will only get you hurt or killed. Do I make myself clear?"

As he glared at me, I nodded.

He pulled into the parking area of the police station and parked. He turned to me and said, "You do understand, don't you, that I'm not going to be able to keep an eye on you all the time." He sighed. "I think it'd probably be a good idea for you to get away if you can. Visit your family or something for a while. Just be available if we need to reach you."

A knock on the window of the cruiser made both Sam and me jump in surprise. It was the policewoman who was signaling us to follow her into the station. Sam said, "Take my advice and go away. You have my number if anything comes up, right?"

Again, I nodded. My thoughts turned to my family. We had lost contact during my years working the streets, and we'd remained estranged. I couldn't imagine the least likely place to go than Idaho and visit my family. I was under enough stress without that.

Sam led me into a different room than the one I was in before. He handed me the forms I needed to fill out and left me alone. In a short while, I finished the paperwork, and the policewoman came to collect the completed forms and hand me my car keys. "We're done with the car. Here you go."

"Thanks," I said.

Her eyes softened. "Take care and watch your step, okay?"

"I will," I answered with more confidence than I felt.

I was pleased to see that my car had been given a quick wash and sparkled in the sunlight. I drove home, and before I parked the car in the garage, I got out to check it for a tracking device. I smiled as I came to the spot Jerome had said most cops used, and I found it fastened there. I removed it, parked the car, and went into the house to pack my things. I'd hide out at the ranch for the time being.

CHAPTER 20

When I pulled into the ranch, I surprised everyone because they didn't expect me until the following weekend. Sarah threw open the screen door and raced down the stairs to greet me, "Auntie Tiff!"

Her greeting brought tears to my eyes, and I hurriedly brushed them away. I wrapped my arms around her. "What have you been up to, Miss Queen Bee?"

She laughed. "Mama bought me a bunch of books and puzzles. Do you want to help me with a puzzle?"

"I would love to," I answered. That was precisely what I needed to get my mind off my dark thoughts. Betsy wore a worried look when she came out onto the porch. She held the door open for Sarah and me to enter the house, and as I passed by, she whispered, "Everything okay?"

I shrugged. "We'll talk later." I'd have to come clean with them what I'd done, and I knew they wouldn't be happy with me.

When Linda heard me, she came out of the Bat Room and asked, "What's up, boo?"

"We'll talk later—just you, Betsy, and me, okay?"

"Sure."

Missy and Sue-Ling came to the front where we stood. "This is a surprise! Is everything okay, Tiff?" asked Missy.

I nodded. I didn't want Missy to get involved in the heavy stuff. She was tending to Sue-Ling, and she had enough on her plate with that. Sarah pulled me to the coffee table, where she had her puzzle spread out. "C'mon, Auntie Tiff."

Sarah was bright for her age and had already passed doing 100 piece puzzles. She was now working on a 250 piece one. I looked at the box to see what the puzzle picture would look like when finished. It looked complicated, and I was impressed that Sarah was even doing it. I thought it was going to be tough enough for me. We sat and got more of the edge pieces done when Missy called us to come for a late lunch.

As we were sitting down, I smiled and asked Sue-Ling, "How's it going?"

She gave a tight smile back. "Okay."

I was relieved that she sounded more upbeat. Missy worked wonders with the women who came through the ranch. Maybe things were looking up, and we could move Sue-Ling along sooner rather than later.

After lunch, Linda, Betsy, and I went into the office. I closed the door and turned to them. "I'm here because I'm in trouble," I said as I sat down to face them. I filled them in on everything I'd done since I'd left yesterday. They reacted badly to my dressing up, trying to get the attention of one of the pimps who ran the streets downtown.

"You've got to be insane!" declared Betsy, cutting to the chase.

"Why would you do something so dumb? I can understand why you wanted to stir things up, but not like that. Well, at least you found out it was Sue-Ling's boyfriend who killed her uncle," she grumbled.

"Whoa, there's more," I told them about the threat written on my car's windshield and the detective's suggestion to get away for a while. That, of course, was against what we all knew was the opposite of what most police insisted you NOT do—leave town.

"Why would he tell you to do that?" asked Betsy, always suspicious of anything the police said or did.

My cheeks warmed. "I think he was trying to keep me safe … said I was free to get away as long as I was available."

"Humph," said Linda, who didn't trust any man except for Jerome. "He doesn't know you're here then, right?"

"Of course not. I even removed the tracking device from my car that the police installed when they checked out my car at the station."

"What did you do with it?" asked Betsy.

I started to laugh, which confused them both. I finally was able to catch my breath and sputtered, "I put it on my neighbor's car—the one who is always spying on me."

I began to laugh again, and this time both Betsy and Linda joined in. They had met him once when they'd come to my house, and they weren't a fan of his.

We sobered up quickly when Betsy asked, "Who do you think threatened you?"

"It has to have something to do with Sue-Ling, don't you think?" I asked.

Linda paused. "Let me and Jerome see what the chatter is on the internet. What's her boyfriend's name again?"

"Johnny Wong."

"What have you two been able to find out about the auction coming up?" I asked her.

"We've been able to pinpoint a few spots where they aired their advertising campaigns, but they haven't been consistent. We think we may have found a pattern beginning. As soon as we know more, Jerome will tip off his friend. We've only got a few more days left."

"Are you going to be okay if you're not able to stop it?"

Linda looked grim. "What choice will I have?"

"Didn't you tell us the other day that you and Jerome have been sending untraceable emails to people in positions of power here to alert them to what is going on?"

"Yeah, for whatever good that is. The only thing that actually works is to take down the pimps. Without the pimps or buyers, most of what's happening on the streets could be cleaned up," stated Linda.

"And that goes for all human trafficking—no buyers, no trafficking," said Betsy.

"If it were only that simple ..." I said.

CHAPTER 21

I left the girls and went to change into my jeans and head to the barn. "Hi there, big girl. Do you feel like a little run today?" I threw the saddle over Big Red and led her outside. When I saw Scout trotting our way, I hollered to Missy and Sue-Ling to call him, not wanting him to tag along.

It was amazing the feeling that overcame me each time I sat high in the saddle on Big Red and rode as one with the wind blowing in my face. It was so exhilarating! For those rare moments, it helped me clear away the cobwebs and worries and allowed me to be free without any plan. We raced along and were turning to go up to my favorite spot overlooking our little valley when I noticed someone had beat me to it. I couldn't make out who was sitting there, but I continued up anyhow. As I came closer, it was when he turned around that I recognized who it was—Rick from the nearby ranch. His eyes lit up when he saw me, and I felt a rush of pleasure.

"Hi there, neighbor," greeted Rick.

"Hi there yourself," I said as I dismounted and draped the reins over Big Red's head. "What are you doing here?"

"Taking a break. Glad you're here, though," Rick added with a flirtatious smile wide enough to entice a fly into a spider's web.

"Really," I said, playing along. "Now, why would that be?"

"It's always good to get to know your neighbors, don't you think?"

"Maybe," I laughed as I sat down next to him and faced the valley below. "So tell me about yourself. How come I haven't seen you around before this?"

"When I graduated from Harvard, I decided I liked living in the northeast. I moved to Boston and got a great job doing PR work for nearly 15 years. When my dad got sick and needed my help, I came back here to become a rancher."

"I didn't know your dad was sick!"

"Heart. He's had two small heart attacks already, and I'm here to take some of the stress from his life before he croaks. He deserves that after all he's done for me."

"Yeah, he's a good guy. How are things going?"

"Well, we've still got a few sheep left, but we've cut the horses down to six now—just the stallion here and the five mares we've had for a time now. We kept them for riding except for our two broodmares. Dad still gets requests for our foals. Nice, huh?"

"Yeah, I love Arabians; they're so beautiful. But I'll take my quarter horse here any day. Right, Big Red?" On cue, she nickered behind us, and Rick and I smiled at each other.

"What about you, Big Red?" he teased, calling me by his dad's nickname for me.

"My friends own the ranch and let me stay there when I want to get away."

"That's it?"

"Yeah, pretty much," I answered as I rose to escape him.

"Hey!" he hollered as he joined me. "Want to go for a beer or two?"

"Not really," I answered truthfully.

He looked taken aback, and I realized I needed to clarify my answer. "That sounds nice and all, but I don't drink. Sorry."

"Maybe dinner sometime?" he pursued.

"Maybe ..." I mounted Big Red. "See you around." I trotted off, leaving Rick behind. I had no intention of dating anyone, least of all, my neighbor.

When I reached the bottom of the ridge, I dug in my heels and gave Big Red a nudge, and we raced across the flatter land, away from the mountain. I hadn't been down that way in quite a while, and I was delighted to become lost there with no one else around. Its solitude made me feel unfettered from worry. As we rode back nearer to the ranch, though, my thoughts darkened and turned inward.

I thought about Sam and Rick. Both showed an interest in me. As a teenager, I would've jumped at the chance to go out with either of them—or any man, for that matter. It had taken time and therapy to realize my need to be loved had to begin with me loving myself. I was still working on that. I wasn't sure I was emotionally ready to get involved romantically with anyone. And it was a good thing I didn't need to make a decision anytime soon. I didn't yet trust myself to make a good one. The last romantic decision I'd made nearly cost me my life. It had started badly and had ended badly.

> When Roger strolled her way with that smooth masculine swing of his hips in tight jeans that screamed, "I am man," she had been blown away that he had chosen her for the next dance. Every female eye in the full room of people was watching her with envy as he held his hand out to her. When she paused, he quickly grabbed her hand, intending to lead her onto the dance floor. "Hey, beautiful."
>
> She was barely able to overcome her infatuation enough to squeak out, "H…Hi."
>
> As he continued to pull on her, he forced her to rise from her seat. As she did, he jerked her arm and pulled her forward, plastering her body against him. A jolt of electricity raced through her when she felt his manhood as he pulled her even closer. It was hard for most people to believe she was naïve being in the business she was.

But the truth was that she was inexperienced dealing with men, not having had much practice. She smelled his beer breath and turned her head away. She knew he was trouble. "I don't dance," she said to him as she tried to sit back down.

"Well, now you do," he growled, annoyed that she'd rejected him.

Before she knew it, their relationship had progressed to the point where she was torn between loving him and hating him.

I shook myself free from my thoughts and turned Big Red toward home, where just the idea of the ranch being my home boosted my spirits.

CHAPTER 22

As soon as I arrived back at the ranch, Betsy walked out to greet me, and I dismounted. "We've got a problem. After you give Big Red a rubdown, meet us in the Bat Room."

She left in a hurry, and I began my tasks with Big Red. As I brushed her, I apologized. "I don't mean to give you the rush, but I need to see what's going on."

As I stepped into the Bat Room, Betsy walked forward and immediately closed the door behind me. We headed to where Linda and Jerome sat, looking grim. Linda held out Sue-Ling's phone. "Here. Read this."

I read the text and shivered. **I know where you are and I'm coming to kill you.** Is this text from Sue-Ling's boyfriend?" I asked.

They nodded.

"Do you think it's true, or is he just trying to scare her?" I asked.

"Who knows?" said Linda in disgust.

Just then, my regular cell phone rang out its song. The four of us stood there in surprise. I didn't usually get calls on my cell phone because clients only had my landline number. The only people who had my cell phone number were standing before me. I reached into my back pocket and pulled out my phone. When I saw who it was, I grimaced—Sam Miller. I didn't answer it. I had no desire to speak with him. If he left me a voicemail message, I'd find out what he wanted. A few seconds later, my phone chirped to tell me I had a message. I put my phone on speaker and played the message for all to hear.

"Hello Tiffany, this is Sam calling to tell you we know you put your tracer on your neighbor's car. That wasn't very smart; now we can't help keep you safe." He sounded exasperated with me, but oddly as if it were someone in a more intimate relationship might sound. "Remember, if you need me, call me or call me anyhow, hear?"

My face reddened as I saw the expressions on the faces surrounding me. "So, it's Sam now, is it?" asked Betsy.

"Don't read more into it than it is. Sam doesn't want anything to happen on his watch is all," I protested.

"Yeah, right," interjected Jerome with a chuckle.

"Let's get back to our problem," I demanded. "What are we going to do now about Sue-Ling's threat? We knew we couldn't keep the ranch secret forever, so are you thinking he knows where she is, and he'll come hunting for her."

They nodded in reluctant agreement.

"Betsy? Does your sister still own that cabin at Keuka Lake?" Betsy's sister was the only one of her siblings who was on speaking terms with her and had shown up a year or so ago wanting to be a part of Sarah's life.

"Yeah, she wanted us to visit this summer, but I put her off."

"Here's what I suggest. Leave tonight. Take Sarah, Missy, and Sue-Ling with you. Once there, pass Sue-Ling onto the rehab that promised a bed for her by the end of the week."

Sensing the reality of Sue-Ling's text message, we were quiet. "I mean it. Get packing and leave tonight. We'll hire a driver to take you to Salt Lake City, and you can catch a plane out of there," I urged.

"I can't leave you and Linda here by yourselves!" exclaimed Betsy.

"Yes, you can," chimed in Linda. "We've got animals to care for, and I can't let my equipment get destroyed. We'll be fine." Turning to Jerome, she said, "It's up to you whether you want to stay or not."

"Well, I'm not leaving you girls alone," he said, angry to think we thought he might leave.

"All right, then. Get going," I ordered.

After Betsy left, I turned to Jerome. "Where do we stand on the alarm system?"

"The equipment should have been delivered to your house already. I went into North Las Vegas yesterday and bought the wire. We started laying it out last night."

"Don't you two ever sleep? Okay then. After dark tonight, I'll drive to the house to pick up your packages. How many should I look for?"

"There should be two boxes."

"Won't it be safer to have Lester pick them up and bring them here? I'm sure he'd do so if asked. Just give him a call. Remind him to be careful and not followed here," suggested Linda.

"That's a good idea, Linda. I'll call him."

Sarah came running into the Bat Room. "Auntie Tiff! We're going to swim in a big lake. C'mon, we have to pack."

"I'm sorry, sweetheart, but I'm not going. I need to stay here and take care of the animals. But you hurry now and pack. Don't forget to take your pretty new sundress."

She stood and looked at me with trembling lips. "But I want you to come too!"

"Next time, sweetie, okay?"

"C'mon, Sarah," called Betsy from the front room. "We need to hurry."

I stood on the front porch with Linda and Jerome to wave goodbye. As they drove off down the road, part of me went with them. Betsy and Missy had become like cherished sisters to me, and there were no words to describe my feelings for Sarah. This parting was like the expression said—sweet sorrow.

CHAPTER 23

After I tended to the animals, Lester and Lucy arrived with the boxes of equipment they'd picked up from my house. I had fresh coffee waiting for them, and we sat at the kitchen table. Soon, Linda and Jerome joined us.

"I don't like the idea of you three being here by yourself. I'm not sure you're up to dealing with what could easily take place here. Those people in that line of business have no moral compass, and they'll think nothing of hurting you or worse."

"You, of all people, must know I can't take any chances of anything happening to my equipment," Linda beseeched Lester, who had his own stash of techno-toys.

"And the animals have to be tended to," I pleaded. "We can't leave them without food and water."

Lucy listened to what we'd said, then suggested, "Can't you call in the FBI since you work with them, Jerome?" They were in the dark about why Jerome was staying with us.

His eyes widened. "That's not a good idea. They'll take over this place, and it'll never be the same. They'll ruin what you're trying to do here."

"Jerome's right. It's not a good idea at all," seconded Linda.

"We'll be able to finish up the security system by tomorrow, so that will help," said Jerome. "Besides, that text message might be a ruse—his way of scaring her." He paused. "Wonder if we set up a signal to let you know if there's trouble here, and you need to send in the cops?"

"What do you mean?" asked Lester.

"If you give me your cell phone number, I can set it up on Linda's and my computers and cell phones; yours too, Tiffany. If we need to call in help, all we have to do is push the button I set up, and a call will go straight to you, Lester. Even if someone surprises us, it'd be easy enough to push the button on one of our computers or phones before anyone noticed."

"Can you do that?" Lester asked.

"He can do anything!" exclaimed Linda. She lightly punched Jerome's arm as she turned her blushing face away from him.

Jerome's face turned pink. "Yes sir, I can set that up. It'd ring to you, and you'd call the police. The police station usually needs someone to tell them what's going on before they'll do anything. We may not have the time to do that."

"Are you okay with that, Lester?' asked Lucy frowning. "It's easy for you to get caught up in things at the soup kitchen, and you might not hear it."

Jerome immediately piped in, "I can rig it to call your number at the same time as well if you want."

Lucy smiled. "That makes more sense. Between the two of us, we should be able to hear it."

I yawned, tired from the turmoil. Scout was by my side and moved as if to get up, causing Frick and Frack to come running for a pat, not wanting to miss out on any attention. "These three here will be our biggest help since they're pretty good watchdogs," I said as I rose from my seat. "I've got to let the dogs out now and go to bed. I'm exhausted."

Lester and Lucy rose, as well. "Are you guys okay if we don't spend the night and head back into town?" Lester asked.

We nodded our okay. When I realized I'd just opted out of helping Linda and Jerome with installing the security system, I changed my mind about heading to bed. "Hey, guys. I'll stay and help you with the security system ..."

"Naw. You'll be in the way," said Linda, winking at me. I smiled, knowing she liked having Jerome all to herself.

After we all said goodnight, I plodded up the stairs with Scout beside me. I felt drained of energy—more tired than I had been in a long time. I did the minimum to ready myself for bed before I slipped under the cool covers, and Scout stretched along the foot of the bed.

I tossed and turned with worry, and even accidentally knocked Scout off the bed with my flailing feet. He twirled around and around on the floor and finally settled there, where it was safer for him. I heard him snoring in peace between the wild dreams that floated in and out of my semi-consciousness. Sue-Ling's face flashed as did Sam's and Rick's. I thought of Sarah and shivered at the thought of anyone hurting her. I couldn't calm my fear or push away a nagging warning that someone was going to die.

By the time I got out of bed the next morning, I was already tired and felt awful. But I forced myself to throw on jeans and an old shirt to head out to the barn to feed the animals. I grimaced as I milked the cows. I wasn't very good at it, and neither the cows nor I were happy about it. But I ended up with a full pail of milk between them, and I proudly headed back to the house without sloshing the liquid over the side.

I put on the coffee and took out bacon from the refrigerator. As I stood at the stove, I looked outside to see that Jerome was headed my way from the shed where he was staying. He appeared as bad as I felt. "Good morning, Jerome. Can I pour you some coffee?"

"Sure. Is Her Highness up yet?"

"Who are you calling Her Highness?" asked Linda as she stepped through the doorway and into the kitchen.

He laughed. "Here, take this coffee. I'll get another one."

I smiled to myself. It looked as if none of us had gotten a wink of sleep. Hopefully, no one would attack the ranch today because I wasn't sure we could even handle pushing a button. "Is the security system in place?" I asked.

"It should be all set. We're going to test it out this morning," Linda said.

"Give me your cell, Tiffany, and I'll set the button up on your phone," said Jerome.

"Why don't you guys take a break and watch a movie or something to relax? You both look done in," I suggested.

"We might just do that," said Linda, looking at Jerome for agreement.

"Sounds good to me. After testing out the alarm system, the other stuff can wait. I think there's a baseball game on."

Linda groaned, and I laughed. I handed my cell phone to Jerome, and as I did, it rang, startling us. Jerome looked at it and smiled when he saw who the caller was. With a raised brow, he said, "It's the detective for you."

I was too surprised to let the call slide, and I answered it instead. "Hello, Sam." I stood in shock as I listened to what he said. With a pounding heart, I sat back down in my chair to collect myself. "Are you sure?" I asked, knowing it was true. "I can't believe it! Yes, I'll be at the station as soon as I can."

Linda was nearly frantic with worry. "What's happened? Are the girls okay?"

I nodded. "It's Lulu. She was found outside the casino, beaten to death. Sam knows that I met with him at the casino that night, and the police need to talk to me. I have to meet them as soon as I can make it there."

"What are you going to do?" asked Linda, upset.

"I'm going to tell them that I wanted to find out about Sue-Ling's uncle and what the word on the street was. Don't worry. I won't have to mention anything about Sue-Ling.

I put my phone into my pocket and went to take a quick shower. I couldn't believe that big, beautiful, black Lulu had been killed. Why?

CHAPTER 24

As I drove closer to the police station, my mind wandered back to the only time I'd spent the night in jail.

"Put her in with the rest of the night stalkers. I'm not letting her out until she sobers up," said the policeman in charge. "Just because she's not one of them doesn't mean she deserves extra accommodations," he added.

Shame covered her entire body like a heavy blanket as she stepped inside the cage that held several prostitutes who'd been pulled off the streets and jailed. She was only drunk, not one of those girls who'd lowered themselves to be bought by any man willing to pay for a trick or two. She'd never let that happen, she vowed at the time.

My thoughts crowded each other as I thought how easily I'd crossed the line to become one of those "night stalkers" when alcohol, combined with the fancy drugs that'd been shared with me, had taken over my life. My need for the drugs outweighed everything else until there was nothing left of my pride, and I'd put myself out on the streets to earn money for the ever-demanding highs that the drugs gave me. I shuttered at the memory.

I thought about the other "angels" and how our backgrounds had been so different. From a young age, Betsy had been sexually abused in her own home and had grown used to men using her for their pleasure. In turn, she had understood the sexual power a woman has over men and learned how to use men for her benefit and gain. Betsy wasn't bitter and didn't carry a grudge about what'd happened to her at a young age. She was pragmatic and did what she felt was best to take care of herself and her daughter, and if that included taking advantage of a man in any way, she'd do so without a second thought.

Then there was Linda. She'd never received the love of a mother—only a grandmother who regularly picked on her for not being the beauty queen she wanted her to be. So Linda made sure she wasn't one by wearing weird outfits, tattoos, piercings, and coloring her wild hair. The incident of watching her girlfriend's peril changed everything for her when she'd been helpless with no power to change what was going on before her eyes. By understanding the power and influence the internet had over our daily lives and learning how to manipulate the data, Linda was able to assuage her guilt by seeking to punish the men who'd killed her friend. She expanded that to include taking on the injustice of how men treated a woman—especially sexually—and retaliated by negatively interfering in their lives via technology. Her pleasure in being able to do so gave her a reason to live. Outside of that goal, she was a tender person with a good sense of humor.

Missy was another story entirely. She had been sex-trafficked at the age of seven and had been used and abused in awful ways. Both genders used her sexually. They beat her and starved her until the day she was found near death in an alley downtown. It was while she spent many weeks in the hospital, healing her broken body and spirit, that she escaped from the reality of what'd happened. She survived by immersing herself in nursing—how the body works and functions. That concentration of looking at the beauty of God's work during her healing period had saved her. She was fragile but steadfast in her belief that everyone deserved love, and she made herself available to those in need who passed through the ranch.

A chill raced down my body. I'd had it easy in comparison because I'd grown up with a reasonably typical home life. My mother and father were still married, happy in their relationship. They had a very strict sense of what they considered to be right and wrong and didn't want me to stray from their belief system. They never would've approved of what I had done, so I was the one who'd broken away from them, too ashamed to face them. I was working on changing that dynamic to heal the rift I'd created, but I still wasn't there yet.

As I pulled into the police station and parked my car, my heart skipped a beat until I reasoned I'd only be there at the station for a short time, and then I could head back to the ranch. I pushed away the memories of years past, and when I walked into the police station, I was surprised to see Sam out front. It appeared as if he'd been waiting for me. "Glad you could make it, Tiffany. C'mon back."

I followed him. Instead of going into the interrogation room as I expected, we went to the back and into his small cubicle, where he offered me the only guest chair able to fit inside the space. I plopped myself down and fought back my tears as I glimpsed the photo of Lulu taken at the crime, sitting on top of his desk. He'd had a rough time of it by the look of things. Sam noticed my distress and flipped the photo over. "So, Tiffany, tell me why you met with Lulu at the casino a few days ago. And I want you to level with me."

"I wanted to hear what the word on the street was about the Asian man who'd come to see me."

"Did you find your answer?"

"Yes. Lulu said that the word was that Johnny Wong had killed him."

"That's what we believe too. Unfortunately, it looks like he's skipped town. By the way, do you know what he looks like?"

I shook my head. "Do you have a picture of him?"

"Yes, and I think it's a good idea for you to study it carefully."

"Why?"

"I'm concerned that you're going to be hurt." Sam shuffled things around on his desk and then pulled up a photo from a stack of papers and handed it to me. "When I looked into your file here, it says you had trouble a few years ago with Blackie. Did you know that he's back in town?"

"I saw his picture in the newspaper a few days ago. Can't you do something about him?"

"We're trying ..."

When I looked at the photo of Johnny Wong, my stomach turned. I knew what he was capable of merely by talking to Sue-Ling. But it was the look in his eyes that scared me. He didn't look right—unbalanced. The thought crossed my mind that he wouldn't think twice about killing us. Goosebumps covered my body as if to confirm my thoughts.

Sam must have seen my discomfort. "Looks like a miserable prick, doesn't he?" Seeing my pink cheeks, he added, "Sorry about the language."

"He's scary, all right." We sat there staring at each other until my stomach fluttered with unease. Something about the way Sam looked at me made me wish for more in my life and better times. "Are we done here?" I asked, breaking the hold we had on each other.

Sam cleared his throat. "We need to discuss something else. I know that you removed the tracking device from your car, and if we put on another one, I imagine you'll probably remove that too. So let's make a deal, okay? Until this thing blows over, I want you to report to me each day. I...we need to know you're okay."

I felt my face warm.

"It's either that or we throw you in jail for your safety," he vowed. "What do you say?"

Although I knew he couldn't keep me jailed, I agreed to his bidding.

"I also understand that you don't want anyone to know where you're staying, so let's make that call once in the morning and again at night, do you agree?"

I hesitated, then thought about the photo of Johnny Wong. By my having to call Sam, it gave Linda, Jerome, and me additional protection if we needed it. I'd explain that to them when I got back to the ranch. "Okay, Sam, you've got a deal," I agreed and rose to shake his hand. When his hand closed around mine, there was a current between us. I knew he'd felt it too, and my cheeks flamed.

As I walked down the hall to leave, Sam was close behind me, his hand at the small of my back. The surge of energy that flowed from that spot throughout my entire body made me tingle all over. By the time we arrived at the front, I knew my face had heated to a bright color that competed with the color of my hair. As I stepped away and turned to say goodbye to Sam, he looked at me with a twinkle in his eyes that softened with desire.

"Take care, Ms. Darling. I'll catch up with you later." He smiled as he noted that my face was reddening even more at the intimacy of his words. I said nothing but simply nodded before I turned to leave.

CHAPTER 25

I decided that as long as I was in town, I'd stop by my house and make sure everything was okay. As I neared it, I saw my annoying neighbor talking to a man standing on my porch, knocking at my front door. I slowed down to see what was going on and froze when I saw it was Johnny Wong. I pressed on the gas at the same time my neighbor recognized me and shouted out for me to stop. He pointed me out to Johnny, who raced down the stairs and hopped onto his motorcycle to chase after me.

I hightailed it down the street and took first one turn, a second turn, and then tore around the third—one right after another—and headed toward a stretch of road where I'd be able to go flat out. I turned onto the road only to find a car right in front of me. I swerved around it amid honking horns and raced to the entrance of Route 215. I stepped on the gas, turned onto the highway, and drove west.

When I looked in the rearview mirror, I saw Johnny's motorcycle gaining on me, and I panicked. I turned off at the next exit and pulled into a professional building situated just off the highway. I hopped out of the car where I'd pulled into the only available space—a handicap space— and ran inside. I looked for a place to hide, and the sign for the ladies' room caught my eye. I popped inside. Immediately, I punched in Sam's number and told him where I was and that Johnny Wong was after me. I hung up as soon as I heard running feet in the hallway and pulled my feet up onto the toilet seat after locking my stall door.

As I sat there with my heart pounding, I heard scuffling outside the bathroom door, and then an irritated voice exclaimed with a huff, "Well, I never!" Through the slot of my door, I saw a middle-aged lady struggle to push an older lady in a wheelchair through the entrance of the bathroom. At the same time, Johnny was trying to get around her to search for me in the bathroom. "I'll call the cops if you don't leave right now!" she threatened in a high shrill voice.

We all heard the sirens as they came closer and closer. "Fuck!" Johnny exclaimed and raced away.

"What a disgusting man," the older woman said to her friend.

When I stepped out of the stall, I startled the two ladies. The older one began to fan herself to settle her nerves. "Are you all right?" I asked. "I didn't mean to scare you."

"It's been quite a day, hasn't it, Flo?" she laughed nervously.

"For sure," confirmed the younger woman.

I left them to wait for the police to arrive. As I stepped outside, two cars came screeching to a halt in front of me: one a patrol car, and the other Sam's everyday police car. Sam got out in a hurry leaving his door open, and stretched himself across the roof of the vehicle. "Are you okay?"

I nodded, glad to see him. "It was Johnny Wong; I'm sure of it. He's on a motorcycle."

"Damn it! We passed one coming out of here." Sam went back inside his car, and I heard him on his radio, calling in a request to track down a motorcycle heading back into town. "If you're okay, I'm going to head out and see if we can get this guy. We'll talk later."

"Go ahead. I'm fine." I walked to my car, and a delayed reaction to my narrow escape started my adrenaline pumping. I placed shaky hands on the steering wheel, drove out of the parking lot, and headed to the ranch. All that'd happened recently was unnerving.

Ever since I'd gotten clean and sober, my life had been pretty calm and peaceful with its fixed routine. Becoming a bonified counselor created plenty of schoolwork to do. My daily routine then had consisted of attending classes, completing homework, and going to AA meetings. That pretty much kept me busy and out of trouble. With Lester and Lucy and the other angels, my living expanded as we helped others get their life straightened out, which until Sue-Ling came to us, had been pretty calm and straight forward.

Things were fine, or so I thought. Yet, what was it about Sam that left me feeling empty, wanting something more? He made me want to prove to him that I was a better person than he had known in the past. And if we were going to share more time through the required check-in phone calls, would I be able to get beyond the shame that seeing him again had brought about? Would he be able to see me in a manner different than what he had known? I'd worked hard to look beyond all my indiscretions, so it shouldn't matter to me what he or anyone else thought about me. Yet, it was different with Sam. I wanted his respect, if nothing else, despite knowing it wasn't to my benefit to look outside myself for approval of any kind. Was he even interested in knowing me as I am now?

I laughed at myself. Jumping ahead, are we, Tiff? Come off it! What was I thinking? Why would Sam be interested in me, anyway? At this point, I was only trouble for him. And did I want to get involved with him at this point in my life? Again, except for the past few weeks, my life for eight years had been pretty terrific and stable. I decided right then it was best to keep it that way without any thoughts of what else could be.

When I reached the ranch, it seemed odd not to have Sarah greet me, and I missed her terribly. True to his nature, Scout wandered out to greet me, and I hugged him a bit tighter than usual. He looked at me, puzzled. "I just needed an extra hug," I said, and he wagged his tail. "C'mon, let's go inside."

Walking into the living room, I saw Linda and Jerome on the couch leaning into each other, sound asleep with the television going. The baseball game was ending, so I checked the score in case they woke up and asked me who'd won. I went into the kitchen and began to sort through the freezer to see what I could fix for dinner later. I took out pork chops that I'd grill along with fresh asparagus. Then I slipped out the back door and headed out to the barn. I looked to see where the two of them had attached the cameras, and I couldn't see any. I stepped closer and searched higher, and I was surprised to discover them tucked away, much smaller than I would have imagined. Like all the techno-toys that seem to shrink in time, these weren't more than an inch across.

The cows mooed, and the horses neighed as I entered the barn, and their greetings made me feel even more protected knowing we had extra "watchdogs" on the alert for anyone who came around. I went into the stall where the cows were waiting for me to milk them. It had been a while since I'd helped Missy with that, and they looked at me with misgiving. I laughed at their doubtful expressions and pulled up a stool. Missy had shown me what to do with the milk if I wanted to make cheese, and I thought I might try my hand at it. What the heck, why not?

Afterward, I checked on the hens. Now that they'd finished the corn I'd thrown them earlier, I gathered the hens into their house, with them complaining and scolding me every step of the way.

Next, I went to the horses. Big Red and her baby of seven years pushed their noses into my pockets, seeking the apple I'd cut up for them. I gave in and fed them one slice at a time. Then I mucked out their stall and put fresh hay down, and left.

Afterward, I was tired and drained of energy. I planned to start dinner and go to bed early. I wasn't sure if sleep was going to be possible if my mind stayed crowded with the vision of Johnny Wong's unpleasant face.

Linda came into the kitchen as I set the cow's milk down and washed my hands. "Hi there, Tiff. How did you make out at the police station?"

"The cops think Johnny Wong is the one who killed Lulu too. I got to see a close-up picture of him and man! He's one scary dude."

"No surprise there," said Linda.

"I thought as long as I was in town, I'd check on my house. When I drove by, guess who was on my porch, knocking on the front door?"

"Who?"

"Johnny Wong!"

"You've got to be kidding!"

"My annoying neighbor pointed me out to him, and he hopped on his motorcycle and chased after me. Once on 215, I could see him gaining on me, and I panicked. I got off Exit 33 and ran inside the professional building there, and hid in the ladies' bathroom. I thought it was all over when I heard Johnny outside the bathroom door, but then I was saved by two ladies who were entering with a wheelchair. They blocked him. I'd already called Sam to let him know what was going on, and Johnny left as soon as he heard the police sirens coming that way."

"Thank God, you called Sam."

"I'm afraid, though, Linda, that Johnny Wong isn't going to rest until he tracks down Sue-Ling. He thinks I know where she is. I hate putting you and Jerome in danger ..."

"Putting who in danger?" asked Jerome as he came into the kitchen.

Linda began to explain what'd happened, and I left them to start preparing dinner. As I stood at the sink, trimming the asparagus stalks, I felt Linda's arms go around me for a squeeze. "We've got you covered, babe. We're not going to let anything happen, okay?"

My eyes watered, and I turned around. "Thanks, Linda. I don't know what I'd do without you and our other angels. Lester and Lucy too."

"We make a good team, don't we? And now we have Jerome here too," she said as she turned to him with a shy smile.

"Yes, Jerome, I'm grateful you're here as well," I amended.

Jerome smiled broadly. "Anything for the Angels."

"Have you taken care of the animals yet?" asked Linda.

"All but the dogs. Can you handle that?"

"Sure. C'mon, gang. Time to eat," she called out to the dogs. They scrambled toward her, crowding her as she opened the pantry door and reached inside for their food.

As I stood outside grilling our meal, my mind was stuck on the fact that we were in danger. No information was private today—at least not for long. So the odds were that it was only a matter of time before Johnny Wong or others discovered our ranch and what we were doing—the gap between regulated rehabs and safe-houses that didn't have room for emergencies. We did nothing illegal despite our operation being 'under the radar' so to speak. The single requirement of anyone who stayed with us was to take an oath of secrecy about the location of the ranch and who was involved.

So far, the only exception to what we had set up was Sue-Ling. We had not vetted her as we usually did others. Lester had reacted on an emotional level, wanting to save her without thinking beyond that. I was angry about it, which I knew didn't do anyone any good. More than that, I needed to work harder to become more objective with Sue-Ling's situation and work with the reality of the situation.

Should I leave the ranch and go somewhere else to protect the others? What would that do? It wouldn't protect Linda and Jerome. If Johnny Wong came here looking for Sue-Ling, it wouldn't matter whether I was here or not. They would still be vulnerable and in danger. It was important for the three of us to remain together.

As we sat at the table eating dinner, I teased, "That was quite a baseball game, huh, Jerome? Especially the ending."

He looked at me with a crooked smile. "It was a good thing I slept through most of it since my team lost."

"I think baseball is one of the most boring games there is," lamented Linda.

I laughed. "Sorry, Jerome, I guess I'd have to agree with Linda."

"You two should give it a chance; you don't know what you're missing."

Linda and I laughed together. "I think we both know exactly what we're missing," I teased.

"Yup," agreed Linda.

"Did you talk to Betsy and Missy today?" I asked Linda. "How're they doing?"

"Actually, very good. Sue-Ling seems to be behaving, and Sarah is having the time of her life swimming in the lake. Betsy says she's like a fish in water, and she's learned to dive."

I smiled at the thought. I looked at my watch and realized it'd soon be time for me to call Sam. My stomach flopped, and I groaned.

Linda asked, "Are you okay?"

"Yeah, fine. It's time for me to call Sam, that's all."

"Why don't you go ahead? Jerome and I will clean up."

"Okay, I'll head up to bed then. Wake me up if anything happens, okay?"

"You'll be the first to know," she grinned.

Scout trailed after me as I climbed the stairs. I got ready for bed and climbed under the summer blanket while Scout found his spot at the foot of the bed. I leaned the pillows against the headboard and dialed Sam's number.

The phone rang and rang with no answer, and just when I thought voicemail would kick in, I heard, "Hello?"

"Sam, it's me, Tiffany."

"What time is it?"

"By the sound of your voice, I'd say it's time for bed. Are you okay?"

"Sorry, I must have fallen asleep. Is everything okay where you are?"

"Yes. Were you able to catch up with Johnny Wong?"

"No, but don't worry. We'll get him."

"That's too bad. Okay then, I'll check in tomorrow morning."

"You don't have to rush off the phone. I'm awake now."

"It's me who has to get to bed. It's been a long day."

"Okay. Goodnight, Tiffany."

"Goodnight, Sam," both of us sounded more like the Walton family did when they said their goodnights at the end of their TV show. I smiled as I heard Sam chuckle.

CHAPTER 26

I opened my eyes to bright sunshine and Scout stirring, a low growl rumbling deep in his throat. Wondering what was bothering him, I jumped out of bed and went onto the deck to take a look around. The cows were mooing, impatient to be milked, and let out of the barn. "It all looks good, boy. I don't see anything to worry about."

I jumped into the clothes I'd worn yesterday and headed downstairs. As I raced through the kitchen, I looked around to see if anyone else was up. It was strange to feel all alone in a place where someone was always around, and I didn't like the emptiness. It was always more gratifying to see Sarah at the kitchen table with her cocoa and hear the other angels doing their own thing. Even though I lived alone during the week, it was different there. Probably, it was because I didn't expect anyone to be there.

I hustled out the door with all three dogs following me. They raced around, happy to be outside, while I went to the hen house first. I gathered the eggs, left the door open to let the hens cluck around in their outdoor caged area, and tossed them their food. I took the eggs back inside and fed the dogs.

Back in the barn, I tossed some hay down for the horses and made sure they had water. Then I surprised the cows once again as I pulled up the stool to milk them. As I sat there pulling on their teats, I had a much higher respect for all Missy did at the ranch. I knew how helpful it was for Missy to keep busy, but still.

I took the milk inside and left it on the counter. When I went back outside, Scout followed me into the barn. "Good morning, Big Red and Baby!" Baby was the name Sarah had called the foal when she first learned how to talk, and it'd stuck. "C'mon, let's go outside so I can clean your stall."

As I was leading them outside, I heard the alarm beeping. I opened the gate to the paddock and slapped Big Red's butt, encouraging her to hurry inside. Baby followed at her heels. As I headed back to the house, both Linda and Jerome greeted me at the door, pushing me inside. We rushed to the computer to see what the camera would show us. We watched a horseman approach, and as soon as he came closer, I knew who it was—our next-door neighbor.

"That's Ben, our neighbor. I wonder why he's here. Last I heard, he was recovering from two heart attacks. I'll go check."

Linda and Jerome nodded in agreement, and I stepped out.

"Hi there, Ben. What brings you here to this neck of the woods?"

"Hi there, yourself, Big Red. I was hoping you'd give me a hand. After my last heart attack, I don't like to ride by myself, and I was wondering if you'd come with me up the mountain. I'm pretty sure I know where that coyote has been hanging out, and I'd like to get rid of him if I can. He's been after my sheep, and I can't afford to lose any."

I was torn. I wished Betsy were here because she'd have no qualms about going after the coyote. I, on the other hand, hated killing anything but spiders. I had an unreasonable fear of them. "Where's Rick?"

"Had to go back east and straighten a few things out where he used to work."

"Oh … well, I guess I can help you out. Let me tell the others what's happening. Why don't you get Big Red out of the paddock, and I'll be right back."

He dismounted and headed to the paddock while I went inside. When I came back out, Ben had the horse in hand, leading her into the barn so I could saddle up. My heart thudded because I didn't like the idea of killing the coyote, but I also didn't want it to kill any of Ben's animals—or ours.

As I mounted, Scout barked furiously at the back door, wanting out. I'd asked Linda and Jerome to keep him inside because I didn't want him to get in the way. We left the ranch and headed out under a clear blue sky and a few puffy, white clouds.

"So how are you feeling, Ben? Honestly?"

"Those two episodes were just warnings, the doc says. I've had to change the way I eat, which means no red meat, and that is no way for a man to live," he said disgustedly.

"Ah, Ben. It beats the alternative, though, right?"

Ben smiled. "Yeah, for sure."

"I bet you're happy to have Rick back here to give you a hand."

"Yes, and no. I'm happy to have Rick back, but I'm just not sure it's the right thing for him. But he says he wants to give ranching a try, so I'm letting him."

"He seemed happy enough when I ran into him the other day."

Ben looked at me curiously as we rode side by side at a slow pace. "So what about you, Big Red? What's going on with you? Still having girls come through the ranch?"

Ben knew what we were doing even though, in the beginning, we'd had no intention of sharing that information with anyone outside ourselves.

Several months after the four of us angels had settled in, Betsy hollered, "Someone's coming! Where are Lester and Lucy?"

They came forward, and we all watched the

horseman come nearer. Lester said, "All of you, wait back here, and I'll go see what he wants."

Ben reined in his horse and scowled as Lester came down the stairs to greet him. "I'm looking for the owner," he demanded.

"Well, you're looking at him. What do you want?"

Ben seemed surprised. "I heard there was a new owner, and I wanted to make sure he knew where his land ends and mine begins. The previous owner never got that through his thick skull. I've put up a fence now, but the damn jackass who put it in placed it partially onto your land. I need to show it to you, and if you agree to sign a release form, I won't have to move my fence."

It was easy to see that Lester enjoyed having the upper hand, and Tiffany couldn't blame him. Lester's dark color automatically made him a second-class citizen among many white people, and that did not sit well with him. "I should probably talk to my lawyer first," he drawled, delaying any answer.

"Don't you even want to see what I'm talking about?" asked Ben, surprised.

"Before that happens, why don't you come inside and meet everyone, so you'll know who we all are?"

Disgruntled, Ben dismounted. As he stepped through the door, Lucy stepped to Lester's side. "This is my wife, Lucy. Let me introduce you to the others who'll be living here. Linda, Missy, Betsy, and Tiffany."

Ben shook their hands, and politely said, "It's nice to meet you all."

Ever the hostess, Lucy asked, "Coffee for everyone?"

They all sat at the large kitchen farmer's table, and Ben squished his large frame into the seat next to Tiffany. Missy got up and brought a cake to the table that she'd baked earlier. Then she went back for plates and forks. Missy couldn't have chosen a better thing to have done. As Ben bit into the cake, he let out a pleased sound. "I haven't had a cake this good since my wife died."

And that was all it took to break the stiffness. We began to relax, and Lester, with his gift of conversation, had Ben spellbound with his story. Then Ben told them about his ranch and what he was trying to do by raising some cattle, some sheep, and a few hens. He offered us gratis a couple of cows he had intended to auction off and a few hens. Missy spoke right up. "That'd be wonderful. We'd love to have them."

Ben smiled at her enthusiasm. Lester looked thoughtful. "Let's make a deal. I'll have Tiffany ride out with you to look at the fence so that we can say we checked it. I'll have my lawyer make up an agreement, which I will gladly sign if you keep your promise of what we're doing here confidential, just among us. Lucy and I want to protect the girls as much as possible."

Ben stood up and held his hand out. "You've got a deal." He looked at Tiffany, "C'mon, little lady, let's take a look at that fence, shall we?"

It was after Tiffany called her horse by name that Ben had laughed. "Big Red on Big Red." His joke remained to this day.

In answer to Ben's question about new girls, I said, "Yes, we still do but not as many as before. We've got one with us now."

"I haven't said a word to Rick about what you girls do, although he asked me a lot about you the other day. I think he's smitten."

"Well, I'm not interested in any relationship at this time—with him or anyone."

"I figured."

I didn't know what he meant by that, but I didn't have a chance to ask him because I heard Scout panting behind us as he ran to catch up. "Damn, he must have escaped." I pulled up to wait for him.

"He likes to be where you are, that's for sure."

We watched him make his way toward us, wearing a wide doggy smile. My heart tugged at seeing him. I loved him so much. "Slow down, Scout. We'll wait for you."

We slowly made our way up the mountain. When we reached my favorite spot, I dismounted and dropped the reins over Big Red's head. I got out the water I'd brought with me and poured some into the dish I always carried for Scout. I handed Ben his bottle of water and then gulped mine down. I had a bad feeling that I couldn't shake off.

"We can leave the horses here and walk to where I think the coyote hides, suggested Ben."

"Where's that?"

"You know the small caves to the left of here? I think that's where he is."

"I don't like this, Ben."

"Why don't we just take a look and see."

Ben started trudging further up the hill. I was unhappy about being there and became more agitated when Scout began to whimper, standing beside me, not moving. "What's going on, Scout?"

I reluctantly followed Ben up the hill. Scout trudged beside me, growling low, and when we came upon Ben, he held his arm straight out, signaling me to stop. The sound of a twig snapping came from between the rocks that held one of the small caves Ben had mentioned.

Without warning, a mountain cat wandered out and saw us. She growled and hissed, and when Ben made a move toward his gun, she leaped toward him.

From that point onward, everything happened as if in slow motion. I picked up a rock and hurled it at the cat. It hit her at the same time Ben stumbled and fell backward with his gun cocked, ready to fire. Then, Ben's weapon went off, resounding throughout the small valley below. The cat turned and hightailed it back to the cave, while Scout yelped. When I turned around, I saw blood on his coat as he fell to the ground.

"Oh, my God!" I screamed and raced to Scout's side. He was panting and whimpering.

I looked to where Ben lay. He was out cold, and I was terrified he'd had another heart attack. I poked at Scout's wound. It didn't look deadly, but I wasn't a vet. "Don't move, Scout. I mean it. Stay."

I ran to where Ben lay motionless. I put my finger against his neck and breathed a sigh of relief when I felt a pulse. "Wake up, Ben! We've got to get out of here now." I shook him enough to jostle him awake. "Are you okay? Do you have any chest pains?"

He shook his head, indicating no pain and got up, resting on his elbows. "What happened?" he asked groggily.

"Hurry, Ben. We have to get out of here now. Scout's been shot, and we need to get him to the vet."

"Shot? How did that happen?"

"When you fell, your gun accidentally went off, and he got hit." He stared at me, dumbfounded, and turned to where Scout lay. "Let's go, Ben!" I urged as I tugged on his arm.

He hoisted himself up and went to Scout. "Damn, I'm so sorry, boy." Ben poked at the dog's wound and said, "Thank God. I don't think it's that bad. Here, let me lift him. I'll put him up with you on the horse. I'll call the vet and have him meet us at your ranch."

With tears streaming, I cuddled Scout against me and held onto him as tight as I could. We galloped back to the ranch using the smoothest gait that would also get us back there the quickest way.

Ben was ahead of me, and when he reached the gate, he dismounted and opened it for me to enter. Then, he reached for Scout and carried him inside the house where both Linda and Jerome were waiting for us in the kitchen. Riding back to the ranch, we'd set off the alarm, so they knew we were coming. When Linda saw that Scout was bleeding, she began to tear up. "My God! What happened?"

"Everything happened at once. A mountain cat lunged at Ben. He fell, his gun went off, and the bullet accidentally hit Scout."

The doorbell rang. "That should be the vet," said Ben.

Jerome said, "I'll get it."

As the vet examined Scout, we huddled around him until he looked up at us and demanded, "Back up, guys. You need to give me room to see what's going on here."

"Is he going to be alright?" I asked, fear in my voice.

"He's one fortunate dog. The bullet went all the way through the area between his neck and withers without hitting anything. I'll clean out the wound, stitch him up, and give him a shot to sleep. He should be better within a few days. You'll need to keep an eye on him, though. We don't want any infection setting in. I'll want to see him in a week."

Now that I knew he was going to be okay, I sobbed without shame.

CHAPTER 27

That evening, I stayed by Scout's side until Linda came to me. "Tiff, I know you're worried about Scout, but with you checking on him all the time, how is he ever going to get any rest?"

We both smiled at the truth of what she'd said. "I know. You're right." I reached forward to pat Scout on the head. "Stay right here, Scout. Hear me? Close your eyes and get some sleep. I'll see you in the morning, buddy." My legs had become stiff from squatting down beside Scout, and I struggled to rise.

"C'mon, I'll help you up," said Linda as she pulled on my arm.

"Anything going on with you and Jerome?"

"What do you mean?" she asked too quickly.

I laughed. "I mean with the auction."

"Oh," she blushed. "Nothing new there. We've been able to disrupt some of their advertising, but we're not going to be able to stop the auction from taking place. It'll still happen over the internet. We don't have any idea where the girls will be handed over, either. It's all so disheartening."

"I'm so sorry," I said, patting her arm.

"Well, that hasn't stopped me from being busy, though," she said with a mischievous grin. "I've had time to do some research on your boyfriend."

"Boyfriend? What are you talking about?"

"Samuel Miller, silly."

"What about him?"

"Did you know that he spent three years in Afghanistan and earned all kinds of hero metals? He was wounded twice and came home for good two years ago. He re-joined the police force here less than a year ago as a detective. Pretty interesting, don't you think?"

"I'll say." I wondered what'd happened to him in Afghanistan. I hated war and found it difficult to reconcile it with anyone who'd taken part in it. My heart twisted at the thought of him injured. I looked at my watch. It'd soon be time to give him a call.

"Don't you have a lecture this weekend at UNLV? What are you going to do about it?"

For the past few summers, I'd been honored by being asked to take part in a Counselor's Weekend Retreat held every year to discuss how we as counselors could help our clients caught up in addiction, both in substance intake and addictive behavior. This year one of the main topics to be discussed was the addictive behavior of using iPhones. We already knew the dangerous effect of overplaying video games, and now, even more people were struggling with being addicted to their phones. I was heading up the panel to discuss that problem. I shrugged. "I guess I should let Sam know."

"So, you're going to do it?"

"Why not? I can't stay hidden forever."

"I guess …"

I grabbed a bottle of water from the refrigerator and climbed the stairs to my bedroom. I sat on my deck, lost in thought until the darkening sky reminded me to make my call to Sam.

"Miller here."

A typical response for a cop to answer with his last name. "Sam, it's me."

"Hey, how're things going, Tiffany?"

"Good, I'm letting you know that I have a speaking engagement at UNLV this weekend."

"What do you mean?" After I explained, he asked, "Is your name listed on any of the marketing materials?"

"Probably. Why?"

"I don't like this. Your exposure there puts you in grave danger."

"I can't believe Johnny Wong would even know anything about the seminar," I protested.

"Believe me, if someone is on the hunt for you, they'd know."

"I have no choice but to be there, Sam. They're counting on me, and I'm not going to let them down."

"Can't they find someone to replace you?"

"Wrong question to ask, Mister," I teased.

"I know. You're irreplaceable, right?" He sighed. "What time are you supposed to be there?"

"One o'clock until around four."

"I guess that decides it then. I'll go with you."

"What do you mean, go with me?"

"You are under my charge, so I'll go with you to the event. I'll pick you up, and we'll go together."

"No, I'll meet you there."

He sighed, frustrated. "How about if we meet at the station? I think that'd be the safest place, don't you? And Tiffany, do you have any wigs? You'll want to cover up that red hair of yours. It's a dead giveaway." He paused. "Poor choice of words."

"Don't worry; I'll come up with something."

"Okay, then. Goodnight, Tiffany."

"Goodnight, Sam. Talk to you in the morning."

I thought about Sam attending the event with me. I'd certainly feel safer with him by my side, and it'd be interesting to see what he thought about being in a room filled mostly with women of all ages. Probably pretty boring for him.

I heard the clump of Scout's feet slowly mounting the stairs, and I hurried to the door to make sure he could make it up okay. "Oh, Scout, you poor baby.

Couldn't stay away? Come here and let me help you."
I grabbed a beach towel and covered the foot of the
bed and helped him up. I lay with my head next to his
and sweet-talked both of us to sleep.

CHAPTER 28

The next morning, I awoke to the thumping of Scout's tail banging atop the bed, and a crick in my neck from the way I'd slept next to him. It was apparent Scout was feeling better when he gave me a big doggy smile and edged my way. I was relieved. After kissing his head, I slowly uncurled from my position and made my way across to the deck. It was the first light. The sky was heavy with clouds and looked about to burst with rain. I hurriedly got up and dressed so I could take care of the animals before a storm settled into our area. As I went down the stairs, I laid my hand on Scout's back to slow him down. I didn't want him to hurry and slip.

I smelled coffee as soon as I reached the kitchen. Linda was up. "I thought if we hurried, we might beat the storm," she said.

"Great. Do you want to take care of the hens while I milk the cows?"

"Sure. Here, take some coffee with you. Afterward, I'll come to help you with the horses."

"Okay. Is Jerome up yet?"

"Not yet. But he said last night that he wants to help with the animals, so I'll knock on his door in a bit if he doesn't get up by himself."

"Isn't this the night of the auction?"

"Don't remind me. We're stumped on this one. But..."

"But the fat lady hasn't sung yet, right?"

"Right," she answered with a fist raised.

"What's happening with Sue-Ling? Wasn't she supposed to leave for her new destination?"

"Yesterday."

"Boy, I bet Missy and Betsy were relieved."

"They said they were when I talked to them last night. By the way, Sarah asked for her favorite auntie, and I said you'd call her sometime today."

I grinned at her words. Sarah and I had a strong connection—there was no doubt about that. "When are they returning?"

"Sarah's having such a good time; they asked if they could stay another week."

"I don't see why not. It's fine with me. You?"

"Yup. Fine with me."

As I pulled up the stool to milk the cows, they turned and looked at me with boredom as they munched their feed. They seemed to be used to me now as the one to tug on them. Thirty minutes later, I carried the pail of milk into the kitchen. On my way in, I saw Jerome spreading some corn for the hens. "Good morning, Jer!"

"Hey," he said sleepily.

A thought crossed my mind. "Have you heard anything from the FBI yet?"

"Yeah. The FBI wants to meet with me sometime next week. It doesn't look good."

"That's too bad. I hope that doesn't mean you've lost your job."

"That's the least of it."

"Yeah, I know. I'll keep my fingers crossed for you."

"Thanks."

I didn't have a good feeling about Jerome's situation. Would it affect us? Thunder began rumbling, and I hurriedly left the milk on the counter and raced back to the barn to attend to the horses. Linda was already there, shoveling out the muck. I brought fresh hay to the stall before going back for the horses' feed and freshwater. Twenty minutes later, we finished. I had to admit that it wasn't the most fabulous job. I patted Big Red and Baby and gave them each a carrot that I'd grabbed earlier from the kitchen. Drops of rain began to dance on the tin roof of the barn, and a roar of thunder and a flash of lightning made both Linda and me jump. We clasped hands like schoolgirls and raced to the back door of the ranch, laughing. "Just made it!" grinned Linda.

The smell of bacon cooking floated our way, and we peeked into the kitchen and saw Jerome at the stove. "That sure smells delicious," I said.

"I didn't know you could cook," said Linda, obviously impressed.

"I have many talents," he declared with a twinkle in his eye, winking at her.

"I might have to agree with you," she said as she punched him lightly on the arm.

We sat down to eat the eggs and bacon Jerome had fixed for us, digging in like we hadn't eaten for days. What was it about someone else's cooking that made the food taste better?

"So what's going to happen, do you think, Jerome? The FBI can't fault you for helping to bring down human trafficking, can they?" I asked.

"I've committed the biggest crime, according to the FBI."

"What do you mean?"

"I haven't gone through the chain of command …"

"Ohh."

He shrugged. "Oh, well …"

I looked at Linda, who shrugged as well. "We'll have to wait and see."

My thoughts traveled to the two of them. It was apparent something was going on between them. Did that mean that Linda would be moving on? Or was she hoping that Jerome could move into the shed on a more permanent basis? I wasn't sure Lester and Lucy would be happy with that arrangement. Linda was right. Only time would tell.

"I'll clean up, you two. I know you want to see what you can do to upset the auction. So go get 'em!"

They rose, and Linda muttered, "If only ..."

Scout whimpered, and I knew he had to go outside again. I grabbed the giant golf umbrella and opened the door. I stood over him as he did what he needed to do, and we went back inside with wet feet. "C'mon, Scout. Lay down over here, boy."

Frick and Frack went to him and sniffed him. Then, they licked his face—one on each side. As tender a moment as that was, I didn't want them near his wound. I called them, "Here, girls, come for a treat." That's all it took to distract them.

I helped myself to yet another cup of coffee and sat down at the table and punched in Sam's number. "Hello?"

"Hi there, Sam. It's me. Everything's fine here."

"That's good. Just what I like to hear. Listen, I may not be able to go with you to the seminar tomorrow. I have to ..."

I jumped in. "Don't worry about it. I'll be fine."

"Whoa! That doesn't mean I won't have someone else there with you..."

"For heaven's sake," I interrupted. "You don't have to do that. I'll be fine on my own."

"Hey, hear me out, why don't you? I don't want anything to happen to you."

I was becoming annoyed to think that I was under any obligation to him to do whatever he wanted me to do. I'd had enough of that in the past. "Sam, I want you to listen to me. I'll be fine by myself, and that's the end of discussion."

"I can tell I'm going to lose any argument I have with you about this. So let me leave it that if I can make it, I will, okay?"

"Fine. Goodbye, Sam."

I heard him muttering as I hung up. I needed to stand on my own two feet without interference from Sam or anyone. Except for Lester, I knew what happened when I relied on any man—nothing good.

I needed cheering up, and the one person who could do that for me was Sarah. I punched in Betsy's number. She answered in a cheery voice, "Hi there, Tiff!"

"Hi, Betsy. How's everything there?"

"Much calmer now that Sue-Ling is no longer with us. I honestly think there's a chance she's going to make it. She's had enough of a taste to be among other women who get along and don't compete with each other to realize life can be different. Time will tell. What's going on there?"

"Tell Missy that the cows are getting used to me, but it's not like when she's there. I can't sing to them as she does."

Betsy laughed. "I've heard you sing, and I bet they're missing her too."

I laughed. "For sure. Where's that adorable daughter of yours? I called to hear her sweet voice and to find out what she's been up to."

"She's tugging on my arm as we speak. Here, Sarah, Auntie Tiff wants to say hi."

"Hi, Auntie Tiff!"

"Hi, darling girl. I heard you've turned into a mermaid."

Sarah's squeals of laughter made my heart sing. "You're so funny, Auntie Tiff!"

"So what have you been up to?"

"Mommy taught me how to dive! And Auntie Ellen has a boat that we can ride in. Sue-Ling and Missy didn't like it, but I'm not afraid. I like it when it bounces up and down."

"That can be scary for someone who is not used to it. Maybe Sue-Ling and Missy had never been in a boat like that before."

"That's what Mommy said. When are you coming here, Auntie Tiff?"

"I'm afraid I'm not going to be able to make it. But I'll see you soon. So go have fun, and I'll see you in a few days, okay?"

"Okaay," she said, disappointed I'd not be joining her.

"I love you, kiddo."

"Love you too, Auntie Tiff."

Speaking with Sarah always put me in a better frame of mind. I sure did love that sweet little girl.

That afternoon, I reviewed my notes for leading the session on addiction to iPhones at the conference the next day. Afterward, I left my bedroom and went downstairs to check on Scout. He was tucked into his dog bed, sleeping soundly with his legs twitching in a running pattern. Dogs were terrific that way, playing out their dreams.

I heard sobbing coming from the Bat Room, and I hurried there to see what was happening. Both Linda and Jerome were slumped in their seats with eyes glued to their computer screens showing girls—young girls—being paraded around a walkway. Linda's tears trailed her face and plopped unnoticed into her lap while Jerome pulled her close.

"Isn't there anything you can do?" I said in a pleading tone, as frustrated as they were.

"Hold on!" Jerome yelled. "I think we got a hit. Look!"

"Linda straightened up. "Oh my god! I think you're right."

"What's going on?" I had no idea why they'd become excited.

"We just got in through the back door of their site. Now we can try to see where the perps are broadcasting from!"

"Does that mean you'll be able to take them down?" I asked.

"No, but we'll be able to pass on the information to my friend, and then the FBI can takeover," Jerome answered.

I watched as both Jerome and Linda's fingers flew across their keyboards in excitement. "I think I've got it!" cried Linda. "Call your friend now with these coordinates ..."

I felt weak with relief that maybe those girls parading across the screen could be saved from their threatened fate. Linda and Jerome were going to be tied up for the rest of the day, so it was going to be catch as catch can for supper that night. It'd stopped raining, and I headed out to take care of the animals.

CHAPTER 29

The next morning, I awoke to Scout, snoring softly at the foot of the bed. He'd made it up the stairs on his own, and I hadn't wakened enough to worry over his being there. I lay back and thought about what the day would bring. I remembered the first time I'd spoken at the Retreat. I'd been terrified. I hadn't realized then that my personal life and its downward slope was going to turn into the main topic of discussion that day.

The commentator held the microphone in her hand to address the crowd. "It gives me great pleasure to introduce you to a new member in the field of counseling. She's shared some of her personal stories with me, and I hope she's open to sharing some of them with you all. Here to tell you more is Tiffany Darling."

She was speechless for a minute or two until she found her voice. She took a deep breath and began. "I'm not alone when I say that it's truly my pleasure to be here. If you'd told me a few years back that I'd be standing here talking to you..."

She'd been amazed that her story had touched so many people. They'd come up to her after the meeting to congratulate her. She'd flushed with embarrassment at the understanding that any of her success she owed to Lester and Lucy, her two Samaritans. They wanted no recognition for all the lives they touched via the Angels and the financial assistance they gave those struggling to live a healthy, happy life—one without pimps and addictions. They were indeed two of the most remarkable people she'd ever met, much less had the pleasure of working with closely.

I smiled, thinking of Lester and Lucy. I'd see them that night because they were coming to the ranch for dinner. My stomach growled in anticipation of eating the special fried chicken that Lucy was bringing with her. It was my favorite thing to eat.

I got up to take care of the animals and slipped down the stairs as quietly as possible because I knew that Linda and Jerome had not gone to bed until very late. I didn't know if they were lucky enough to stop the auction or not.

"C'mon boy and girls," I said to the dogs. "Let's go out so you can do your thing."

All three dogs followed me and, perhaps, sensing my mood, were quiet for once. I took my time and went to feed the hens first, then the cows. I'd do the horses last. I felt energized by the sweet, fresh smell of the rain that'd passed through during the night. Each day was a new beginning—a refreshing thought.

I passed the time with thoughts about Sam Wilson. What was it about him that had me so bothered? I laughed at the idea of what that might sound like if I were speaking to a professional counselor. But its truth was clear. It amazed me that so many counselors, like myself, were very helpful to those who came to us for assistance; yet, we were not always able to help ourselves. It was somewhat like the psychics able to see things for everyone but themselves.

I was physically attracted to Sam, for he was an exceptionally handsome man—even more so because of his strength and kindness. I was aware he was interested in me, for I recognized the signs. But I was terrified to become involved with him for fear of losing myself in a way that wasn't healthy. I'd worked hard to become less of a people-pleaser, and it felt good to say no. So I was not going to let anyone, Sam included, take me down the wrong path.

I scoffed at myself. The irony of it was that to hold life at bay was not truly living if I were unwilling to accept the gifts that spirit offered. Again, my thoughts went back to Lester and Lucy. Where would I be if I'd walked away from them those years ago?

"Good morning, Tiff!"

I was so immersed in thought that I'd not heard Linda enter the barn, and I jumped a mile when I saw her.

"Gosh, I didn't mean to scare you," she said, biting back a smile.

"No worries. How did you make out last night?"

"We sent in our information, and we watched the sale go on for an hour or so before it finally went blank."

"That's good then, huh?"

"Who knows?" she answered with a frown.

"Linda, what are we going to do about Jerome?"

"What do you mean?"

"Wonder if the FBI threatens to fire him if he doesn't reveal all?"

"I'm pretty sure they can't find anything on his computer. And if they do, he says it still doesn't lead to us. I hope they don't let him go because if they do, word will spread, and no company will hire him."

"That means we get him all to ourselves then?" I smiled. "Lester and Lucy will be joining us tonight. Are you going to ask them if he can stay here longer?"

She blushed. "I was thinking of doing that. Do you think they'd be okay with it?"

"I don't know. Jerome being here seems to be working out okay, but Lester and Lucy are the ones who get to decide."

"Yeah, I know. It's just that they didn't pick me as one of their angels if you remember. I just kinda showed up."

"Wait a minute, Linda. In their minds, Lester and Lucy most certainly *did* pick you as one of their angels. They'd be devastated to hear you question that."

"I guess," she agreed despondently. "Are you ready for your speech today?"

"Ready as I'll ever be. C'mon, let's find Jerome. That'll make you feel better," I said as I put my arm around her shoulder and led her away with me.

CHAPTER 30

Before I left to attend the seminar, I checked on Scout. "You rest, old man. I'll be back later."

I got behind the wheel of my car and plowed through my briefcase to make sure I had grabbed my notes. Then, I drove off and tried to shake off my nerves. I could feel in my bones that something was going to happen. I'd learned to listen to that inner warning and be aware whenever those feelings popped up. As I drove, I hefted my briefcase from the seat next to me and felt the weight of my gun. I rarely carried it and hadn't used any firearm on a person before. For some reason this morning, I'd felt the urge to take it with me.

As I drove closer to the college, goosebumps crawled across my body. I looked around and couldn't make out anything that would've caused them. I pulled into the parking lot and ignored parking the car in the garage there. Instead, I choose to park by the back entrance in a slot reserved for one of the professors whom I knew wouldn't be using it that day.

I slipped inside, holding my briefcase close. The program was already in session as I knew it would be. So I went to the back of the stage and caught the eye of the hostess of the event. We smiled at each other, and then I peeked out from the stage curtains to view the audience. My heart thudded when I saw Sue-Ling's boyfriend standing toward the back with another man. Our eyes locked, and I knew I was in trouble. I searched for Sam. When I didn't see him, my heart fell. The two men started forward. What was I going to do?

I knew what they expected me to do—run. I looked at my watch to see it was exactly 1 o'clock. It was my scheduled time to be on stage. So that's what I did. Much to the hostess' surprise, I stepped onto the stage and walked toward her. Although mystified by my action, she smiled and introduced me to the audience. They stood up to welcome me, giving me another opportunity to search for Sam. Why hadn't I taken his advice and worn a wig? Would that have helped? Too late now.

I saw Johnny Wong and his sidekick stop where they were standing and then retrace their steps to the back of the room. This time, they seated themselves in two of the empty chairs in the last row. My heart pounded when I looked on as Johnny Wong slid his finger across his neck, staring at me.

My attention went back to the table where four other counselors sat waiting for me to open the panel discussion about iPhones and our addiction to them. Each of us was allowed 20 minutes to talk about some of our experiences in dealing with that phenomenon. As I listened to them and asked them questions, I lost myself in the fascination of my work. When I looked out to the audience later, Johnny Wong and his sidekick were gone. What had happened to them? I knew they weren't going to let me go, and my heart raced.

Toward the end of our session, I saw Sam enter the back of the room and wave at me. I nodded my head in recognition. Then in response to a general question regarding addiction, I said, "It's a feeling of being trapped when two or more men come forward and want to confront you or wait in hiding to attack you. Isn't that right, Mary Beth?"

After Mary Beth closed her mouth in surprise and nodded in agreement, she said, "You're right." Bless her heart.

Sam pointed at me and mouthed, "You?"

"Yes, for sure," I added, tipping my head to the back of the stage. "Who out there has questions for the panel?"

The question and answer period got lively, and when I looked to the audience again, Sam was gone. Hopefully, he'd understood what I'd meant. We ended our session and the workshop for the day with the panelists heading down the stage stairs to join their friends. They were clearing out to get to the cocktail/dinner party at the brewery next door. I said goodbye to them and turned to go backstage to gather my things.

When I pushed aside the curtain, that's when I saw Johnny's sidekick lying on the floor, not moving. A strong arm grabbed me and pulled me close. I struggled and began to bite down on the hand that covered my mouth when I heard Sam whisper, "Shhh. It's me."

He pulled me tighter to him and back-stepped us into a small closet space behind the folds of the curtain gathered at the end of the stage. It was just in time as we listened to quick steps coming our way.

"Where the fuck are you? Do I have to do everything myself ..." Feet shuffled. "What the fuck? C'mon, get up! We gotta get out of here now!"

Groaning sounded and then a sharp cry of pain. "Cut it out! I'm getting up!"

"What happened to you, anyway?"

"I dunno. All of a sudden, everything went black. Did Tiffany get away?"

"Don't worry. I took care of her car. She won't be getting far, and we'll get her then."

In protest, I pulled away from Sam, ready to move forward. He quickly pulled me tighter, so our bodies melted into each other. Soundlessly, he whispered, "Don't move." The heat from his body warmed me in many ways, and I relaxed against him to take advantage of having him so close. Fading footsteps did nothing to part us for several long minutes while we became increasingly aware of our nearness.

Sirens sounded in the background, coming closer. Sam was the first to stir. He grabbed my hand and pulled me out of the closet. "You heard Johnny. Let's go check out your car."

As we headed toward the back of the building, we heard motorcycles storm off. We'd missed catching Johnny—again. As I walked toward my car, my mind began to imagine the worst. When I saw four flat tires, I was relieved. I think Sam was too, but that didn't stop him from lifting the hood of the car to check under it for any signs of disturbance. The cops pulled into the parking lot and surrounded us. Suddenly, I remembered that I'd left my briefcase backstage, and leaving Sam to talk to the police, I went inside. I texted Linda to tell her not to wait for me for dinner. I searched for my briefcase and came up empty-handed.

I jumped a mile when I heard Sam behind me ask, "Are you looking for this by any chance?" He held out the briefcase in one hand, the gun in the other.

I blushed and stammered, "Yes... that's exactly what I'm looking for."

"Do you even know how to use this thing?" he asked, holding the gun high in the air.

"I like having it with me is all."

"I have no intention of returning this gun to you unless you agree to go to target practice with me. It's dangerous to have a gun if you don't know how to use it or care for it properly. Where did you get it, anyhow?" My face reddened. I remained silent, but he would have none of it. "Where?"

"I took it from an acquaintance."

"Ah, I see. I've called the tow company to come for your car. They'll drop it off at your house after they fix the tires. It seems you were fortunate because the knife Johnny used looks as if it was a small pocket knife. It won't take much to patch up the tires."

I stood there, gathering my thoughts.

"Listen, why don't we grab a bite to eat, and then I'll drop you off at your house. You can pick up your car there after you hear back from the tow company. The garage said they'd get on it right away." I hesitated, and he urged, "C'mon, let's do it."

"Thank you, that'd be nice."

"Do you like Thai food? There's a new restaurant that's pretty good."

"That sounds perfect," I said, relief washing over me. It was nice to have someone else in charge for a change.

The restaurant was small and intimate. We sat at a corner table, which gave us privacy to talk. Sam had a beer since he was off duty and I had an Arnold Palmer. When the waitress came to take our order, Sam waved the waitress away. "Give us a few more minutes, okay?"

"Take your time, sir," she smiled. "I'll check back with you in a while or just signal me to come."

"So tell me about you," he said, bowing his head closer to mine.

"Why don't you tell me about YOU?" I responded.

He took in a long breath. "Not that much to tell."

"Weren't you in the service?"

"Yeah."

"Afghanistan?" I asked, encouraging him on.

He straightened in his chair. "Yeah, I was there, alright. I don't like to talk about it much. There's not a lot of positive things I can say about it."

"Okay. What made you want to become a cop?"

"Now, there's a story," he laughed. "I had no intention of becoming one, but a buddy of mine was studying to get into the police academy and wanted me to study with him. We did so much studying together that I learned almost as much as he did. So I decided to take the test. The rest is history, so to speak."

"Did he pass too?"

"Yup, with honors," he smiled.

"That's nice for both of you."

"Now, what about you?" he asked, leaning toward me again.

The waitress stepped forward and saved me from having to say anything other than "Yes," when she asked if we were ready to order.

Sam shook his head at me and smiled, knowing I'd been happy for the interruption. "Sure. We'll have the special with red curry sauce. Is that okay with you, Tiffany?"

"Sounds perfect."

The waitress left, and Sam moved his chair closer to me. Not to be completely shut out of asking me questions, he probed, "What made you want to get into counseling?"

I smiled to myself when I realized that if I weren't willing to talk freely, he'd keep asking questions. "I have two extraordinary people in my life who encouraged me to get my degree."

He lifted his brows. "That's nice. You're lucky to have them."

"You have no idea."

He studied me long enough to make me uneasy. "By the way, we picked up a young girl on the street about a week ago who mentioned your name when I asked her why we shouldn't jail her."

"Really?"

"She said she was working with you to understand more about herself and why she was doing what she was doing."

"Yes ...?"

"She said, if Miss Tiffany could change her life, I can too. If you don't jail me this time, I promise you'll never see me on the street again."

"Did you let her go?"

Sam nodded his head.

"Have you seen her since?"

"Just once, then nothing. Do you know anything about that?"

I was pretty sure I knew the girl he was referring to—Brenda. She was scheduled to see me again in a day or two. "Most of my clients come to me with addiction problems, but I can't discuss any particulars because of client confidentiality."

The waitress brought our food, and we both dug in. It was a fabulous meal. Toward the end, Sam asked, "What about your parents? Are they alive, and do you see them often?"

My face burned. "They're alive, but we haven't seen each other for a while. What about you? Do you get together with your parents often?"

"Wish I could," he answered wistfully. "Car crash five years ago."

"I'm so sorry."

"Me, too." His phone buzzed with a text. "It's the tow company. Your car is ready. We'd better go; they're going to meet us at your house."

We pulled up to the house. The car was in the driveway, and the tow truck was waiting for me out front. I paid the bill, and they drove off. I stood alone with Sam, undecided about whether to invite him in or not. He made the decision easy for me.

"Look, something's come up at the station. I've got to go. Why don't I pick you up tomorrow for target practice at 2 o'clock, okay?"

"I'm not sure that's such a good idea."

Thinking I meant for safety reasons, he asked, "Would you rather meet me at the station?"

"It's not that. I don't like guns." I laughed. "Dumb to say that if I have one, right?"

"Listen, I wasn't kidding before. Target practice is the only way you're going to get your gun back, so if you want it back, you need to meet me at the station tomorrow at 2."

I wanted my gun back. I sighed. "Okay, I'll be there."

"Good. See you then."

CHAPTER 31

As long as I was home, I decided to check my mail. I unlocked the front door, turned off the alarm, and was about to pick up the mail spread across the floor when I felt someone behind me. I straightened and twirled face front with my arms upright and my feet positioned in a karate stance, ready to kick out. I nearly fell backward as I abruptly halted my motion and came face to face with Brenda, the girl Sam had discussed at the restaurant. She put her finger across her lips and pulled me away while at the same time, she tugged the door shut.

"Follow me!" she whispered.

I did as she asked, and we quietly raced to the back, behind the garage. We made it in time to be hidden from the car headlights lighting up the area.

"What's going on?" I whispered.

"I think one of the girls must have said something about my meeting with you. Now that I'm trying to get off the street, my pimp has come hunting for me."

We listened to footsteps mounting the porch. There were two sets of them. Since the door was unlocked, they didn't hesitate to go in. Lights turned on, and we heard them thumping around inside. A dog began to bark, and several porch lights went on in the neighborhood. My nosy neighbor yelled into the dark, "I'm calling the police!"

The men heard him and must have decided it wasn't worth the hassle, and we listened as they ran off the porch. Then car doors slammed, and the car roared out of there, but not before a voice from the car yelled at my neighbor, "Mind your own business, motherfucker."

For once, I was glad he hadn't done so. I turned to Brenda, partially hidden in the dark by her brown skin. "So, what's going on?"

"Tiffany, I'm ready to leave all this behind me. I've thought a lot about what you said. Life is too short to be doing this shit," she proclaimed, chin high in resolve.

"So, what are your plans?" I asked as I headed back to set the alarm and lock the front door. I wouldn't worry about getting the mail.

She immediately deflated. "I dunno. I was hoping you'd help me. I know you've helped others before."

"Where are you staying?"

"With a friend, just for tonight. Then I'll have to move on."

"What about after that? Do you have friends or relatives out of state that'd take you in?"

"I've got my family back in Chicago. They'll let me stay with them."

"Is that what you want to do? Go back to your family?"

"Yes, I'll be safe there, and they want me back."

"If I get you an airline ticket and money to get you settled, would you be ready to leave tomorrow?"

Her eyes rounded with fear and excitement as she realized escape was there for the asking. She hesitated as she thought about it. "Yes, I'm ready. I'm ready to do this," she answered, determined.

"Okay then, let's do it. Are you sure you're safe where you're staying tonight?"

"I'll be fine where I am. I've got to straighten out a few things, anyway."

"Are you sure you're going to be okay?"

"Yes, I'm sure."

"Call me in the morning. I'll pick you up and drive you to the airport. Meantime, I'll make your airline reservation. Sound good?"

Tears rolled down Brenda's face. "How can I ever thank you?"

"Just by getting out of this business …" I said as I enfolded her in my arms. "You're strong, and you're going to be just fine. I know it."

"I believe I will be too."

"C'mon, I'll drive you to your friend's house."

I saw my neighbor begin to head our way. We made it out of there before he reached us.

By the time I arrived back at the ranch, the animals had been fed and bedded for the night. I was delighted to see that Lester and Lucy's car was still there, making it easier for me to fill them in on everything that'd happened. Better to do so in person, not the telephone. I wondered if Linda had discussed the possibility of Jerome staying with us permanently, but I didn't want to ask.

As I entered, Scout lumbered toward me with his tail flapping the air. Just by being safe back at the ranch with my friends, I became almost weak with exhaustion over all that'd taken place. It felt as if someone had let out all my air, and I moved slowly forward to greet Lester and Lucy as Linda and Jerome came out to join us.

After I relayed what'd happened, Lester looked concerned. "I'm surprised you didn't bring Brenda here."

"She said she had some things to clear up, or I would have."

Lucy sighed. "These poor girls who get so trapped. There's no easy way for them to get out, is there?"

"Not unless you have good Samaritans like you two to save the day," I answered.

Lester reached for Lucy's hand. "It's only because of our daughter that we can afford to do it."

What a price to pay for losing a daughter. I knew they'd be happy to exchange any settlement money for their daughter's life back without a second's hesitation.

Lucy said, "Tiff, you look as if you're about to collapse."

I smiled. "That's exactly how I feel. If you'll excuse me, I'm going to bed." I rose and padded my way upstairs with Scout following behind.

CHAPTER 32

I hadn't slept well, and I was more than ready to climb out of bed to face the day as soon as there was enough light. I surprised myself by looking forward to tending to the animals. It was comforting to work with them and made me feel that I was helping Mother Nature to take care of her critters. It felt good.

The dogs were lively and raced around outside as soon as I let them out. All three sniffed the air and moved closer to the hen house, whining. As I approached, they parted, and I saw one of the hens hadn't made it inside the small building last night. Instead, it stood inside the outdoor enclosure, ignoring the three dogs. It was a miracle the coyote hadn't gotten it. I wondered if Ben had been successful in trapping and killing the coyote. I'd have to check with him later.

"C'mon, dogs. Leave the hen alone and let's get the others out, okay?" They looked at me as if they understood what I'd said, and backed away as I opened the gate to get inside the pen.

In the barn, the chores for the cows and horses were easy to do, probably because of my new perspective that it was more pleasure than work. By the time I walked into the house with my pail of milk, Linda and Jerome were in the kitchen fixing breakfast. Linda handed me a cup of coffee. She smiled. "Jerome's going to be staying with us a bit longer. I thought you'd like to know."

"That's good news, isn't it?"

"It sure is," Jerome said. "I'm very grateful to Lester and Lucy. They're very special people."

"When is your meeting with the FBI?"

"They'll call me at the last minute. That's the way they work."

I frowned. "Won't the FBI be able to trace you back here?"

"If they don't clear me, I won't return here. That's my agreement with Lucy and Lester."

"Oh."

My cell phone chirped, and I saw it was Sam. It was doubtful I'd be able to join him today for target practice what with helping Brenda out. "Hi, Sam."

"See you at two?"

"Not today; something's come up. Maybe in a few days?"

"You're not completely backing out, are you? You really can't make it today?"

"Sorry, no."

"Okay, then." I was disappointed I wouldn't be seeing him today, which was an unexpected sensation for me.

I hurriedly got to my computer and began to make the arrangements for Brenda's flight home. At the ranch, we kept cash and Visa gift cards on hand for emergencies, such as Brenda's case. We liked to give more gift card money than cash because the dealers weren't interested in gift cards—they wanted cash. Although Brenda was drug-free, I grabbed $200 in bills and $500 worth of gift cards. I could always send more gift cards if needed.

When my phone rang again, I was relieved to see it was Brenda. "Good morning! I've got you a one o'clock flight. I'll pick you up in two hours. Do you need a suitcase? I've got an extra one here, so I'll bring it along in case you do, okay?"

I heard sniffling. "Thanks, Tiffany."

"Good things are ahead for you, girlfriend. See you in a bit."

When I got to her friend's house, it was charming, belonging to one of the women she'd met at church. Brenda was waiting for me and smiled when I handed her the suitcase. I watched as she packed and was touched to see she'd put in one of the books I'd suggested she read. After dealing with Sue-Ling, it was such a treat to see Brenda doing all she could to get herself out of her dreaded state of affairs. I handed her the money and gift cards, along with her flight information and printed boarding pass. She turned away, emotion on her face.

"C'mon, let's go!" I said, pulling on her arm.

When I drove to the departure area of the airport, cars were lined up, unloading passengers. When we got close to the curb, I stopped the car, and we both hopped out and went to the rear of the vehicle. I pulled out Brenda's suitcase from the trunk and handed it to her. She kissed me tenderly on each cheek as her eyes filled. I choked back tears, and we both were silent as we hugged. Words couldn't express what we were feeling. Brenda stepped up onto the curb and walked away through the glass doors of the airport.

A man darted forward, and when I realized who it was, my heart stopped. It was Blackie—the well-known pimp wanted for murder who'd recently returned to town. He was trailing after Brenda. With him following her, she was in serious trouble. I knew he'd have no qualms about hurting her. I left my car running where it was and ignored the traffic cop yelling at me that I couldn't leave my car there. I raced through the door and looked around to see which way Brenda went.

I thought I saw Brenda to my left and raced forward only to discover it wasn't her. I turned back and ran as fast as I could the other way. I yelled, "Brenda! Watch out!" at the same time, a gunshot rang out, and people scattered. Blackie turned around and recognized me.

He held his gun as if to shoot me. The same traffic cop who'd been racing after me tackled Blackie and hollered for everyone to stand back.

I sprinted to Brenda's side. She lay flat on her back, and it didn't look good. I screamed, "Help me! Someone help me, please! Is there a doctor in the house?"

I pushed back Brenda's hair and murmured over and over again. "You're going to be okay. Hang in there."

Her brown eyes pleaded with me to stop. She knew the truth. I watched Brenda's life slowly fade, and in the end, she reached for my arm and pulled me close. She wore a tight smile. "Free at last," she whispered. That was it. She was gone.

I screamed. "NO! You can't die. It's not fair! NO!"

I bent over her, pulling her body into my arms, determined not to leave her. Sobs wracked my body. A cop came and tried to pull me away. I struggled enough to force him to loosen his grip on me. "No! I won't leave her here!

Out of nowhere, I heard Sam's gentle voice. "Tiffany, let go of her. We need to get her out of here."

I rose to my knees and spied Sam's gun holstered at his waist. I reached for it and stood up. "Where is that bastard? Where is he?" I screamed.

Once again, Sam spoke to me in a calm voice, "Give me the gun, Tiffany. Give it to me now."

I stared at Sam's pleading eyes and then at the gun. I slowly handed it back to him. He put his arms around me, and I fell against him and wept gulping sobs. "It's just not fair, Sam. That shouldn't have happened."

"I know. C'mon, let's get you out of here." He pushed my hair away from my face, tucking it behind my ears, and reached for his handkerchief to wipe away my snotty nose and dripping eyes. I was a mess, and I didn't care.

"I have to remain here. Who can I call to come to get you?" asked Sam.

I pulled my telephone from my pants pocket and punched in Lester's number. Sam took it from my shaking hands and talked for me. Afterward, he stayed with me until Lester and Lucy arrived. I knew Sam was curious about who they were, and I was pretty sure he'd made the connection that they were the two people I'd talked about at the restaurant. I loaded into the car with Lucy driving, and Lester got into my car to follow us.

Before we left, Sam bent down to where I was sitting and kissed me on the forehead. "I'll call you later."

Lucy eyed him, then me, but said nothing.

At the ranch, I let Lucy drag me from the car. I had no energy nor desire to move, and she had to use all her strength to pull me out. All I wanted was to sleep and wake up to what'd happened to be nothing more than a bad dream. Brenda *couldn't* be dead. It was her chance to start a new life. It had to be a bad dream; it just had to.

Even when Scout came to greet me, I had no strength to pat him. I stumbled past him and went inside. I crawled up the stairs and fell across my bed, and sobbed and sobbed with disappointment that life could be so unfair. I cried as if I'd never cried before and had saved up all my tears until then. I cried as if my heart would never heal.

A while later, I felt Lucy's hand stroking my back. "Here, Tiff, take this." She handed me a sleeping pill, and I swallowed it even though I hated taking medicine of any kind. At the moment, I didn't care if I ever woke up. Lucy helped me remove my bloody clothes, and I climbed back in bed in my bra and panties. She stayed with me until everything went dark.

CHAPTER 33

The next time I opened my eyes, it was light outside and many hours later. Linda was sitting beside the bed, reading a book. "Hey, Sleepyhead. How are you doing?"

As the memory of what'd happened came to me, I groaned. I turned away without answering. What could I say?

"Betsy, Missy, and Sarah are on their way home. They should be here soon."

"That's too bad. Sarah must be disappointed not to be able to stay longer at the lake," I mumbled.

"I don't think so. Sarah misses her favorite auntie," Linda said sincerely.

"To be honest, I don't know if I'll be good company for anyone—even Sarah. I'm just so angry!" I spat out.

"Angry at the whole fucking world! Why couldn't a girl like Brenda have another chance at life? Why not? Because some bastard wants to *sell* her so he can become rich? And that's fair?" I wiped away the tears and saliva that my hollering had created.

"I can't say anything that even begins to make sense of it all," said Linda with sadness.

Scout jumped onto the bed and nudged me with his nose. He knew something was wrong when I ignored him, and he pushed into me until I raised my arm to rub his head. "It's okay, Scout; it's okay," I said through my tears. He plopped down beside me and began to lick my tears away until I stopped him.

I crawled out of bed and went into the bathroom. As I came back into the bedroom, Linda held up my ringing cellphone and mouthed, "It's Sam."

I shook my head and mouthed, "No, you take it."

"He wants to speak to *you*, Tiffany, and he's not taking no for an answer," she insisted. When she saw how flustered I became, she hid a smile.

"Okay, hand it to me," I said begrudgingly.

When I heard his voice softened with concern, tears slid down my face, and I choked out, "Hi, Sam."

"Tiffany, are you feeling up to coming to the station to answer some questions?"

"I'm not myself right now. Can't we do it tomorrow?"

"Okay." He cleared his throat. "Are your friends with you? Are you someplace safe?"

"Yes, I am."

"I'd like to meet them sometime…"

I didn't know how to respond. "Listen, I'll talk to you tomorrow morning, Sam. I'll make arrangements then to meet you at the station, okay?"

"That's fine, Tiffany. See you tomorrow."

"And, Sam?"

"Yes?"

"Thanks for being there for me. It meant a lot."

"I'd do anything for you. I thought you might already know that."

"Oh."

"Take care, Tiffany."

My face heated from his remark. I looked at Linda and shook my head. "Men ..."

She laughed. "I think you two have got some things to work out."

I surprised her when I tossed my pillow at her, and we both laughed.

"Now that I'm up, I might as well take a shower and see if I can get rid of some of this anger."

Afterward, I dressed to the noise of my stomach rumbling. I was hungry and hoped that my mind would stay away from my dark thoughts long enough for me to keep down anything I ate. With a life of their own, unbidden tears came and went without being encouraged to do so. I'd seen a lot of sad, unhappy things in the past few years, but Brenda's murder seemed to represent all the bad into that one experience. I was grief-stricken beyond expression— and still angry. The only thing the shower had done was to wash me clean.

Later, as I munched on a sandwich I'd made, I heard a car pull into the driveway. It must be the girls, I thought with heart hammering. God! I'd missed them, especially Sarah.

Scout got up and made his way to the front, and I followed behind. Standing on the porch with Linda and Jerome, I watched as Sarah got out of the back seat of the car and raced toward me. "Auntie, Tiff! Auntie Tiff!"

Watching her run toward me, I broke down and sobbed. Linda came and put her arm around me. "It's okay, Tiff."

"I'm so lucky to have her, and all of you, in my life," I sobbed.

"Auntie Tiff, what's the matter? Aren't you glad to see me?"

"That's why she's crying, silly," said Betsy as she hugged Sarah and me together. "Having a hard time, are you?" she asked me. "C'mon, let's go inside."

"Not before I get a hug too," insisted Missy, who'd entered our group.

The four of us women, plus Sarah, huddled together like old times. When I looked across to the car in the driveway, Lester and Lucy stood together, looking pleased. We were their angels, whether we deserved to be or not.

CHAPTER 34

The rest of the day, the travelers were busy unpacking, doing laundry, and checking on the animals. I started to relax as things got back to normal. Not wanting me to be alone, Lester and Lucy stayed with me, not saying much. Lucy eyed me and took in a deep breath.

"It's not easy to let someone go, is it, my friend?" she said.

I just shook my head. "How did you do it? How did you get through the whole ordeal of your daughter's death? I can't even imagine…"

"She almost didn't," interrupted Lester. "Lucy was a basket case."

"What made the difference?" I asked, curious.

Lucy smiled tenderly at Lester. "He said, 'Let's keep Sarina alive.' I got so angry with him when he said that."

Lester chuckled. "She threatened to divorce me! Asked me who I thought I was—God?"

Lucy laughed. "I would have divorced him, too, if he hadn't explained what he had in mind."

"To think that Sarina had been shot as if she were just another girl on the street, without value," Lester said, shaking his head. "After the trial and all the money that we were awarded, it only made sense for us to do what we are doing now in Sarina's name."

Tears came. I was beyond a mess, thinking what would've happened to me if Lester had not shown up that day and saved me.

"Why don't you go rest, Tiff? I'll come and get you for supper," suggested Lucy.

Like a robot, I rose and climbed the stairs to my bedroom. I knew I had to come to terms with why I was so out of control with my emotions. I didn't have the energy to do it now.

Later, my heart lifted as I sat at the kitchen table with all the people whom I loved sitting beside me. Sarah kept stealing glances at me until her mother placed a hand on her shoulder and said, "Sarah, pay attention to what you're doing."

"Mama, what's wrong with Auntie Tiff?"

The table became silent, waiting for Betsy's answer. "She's very sad. A friend of hers died."

"Oh."

Missy changed the subject. "After dinner, do you want to help me with the animals, Sarah?"

"You'll come too, Auntie Tiff, won't you?"

"Yeah. It'll be just like old times, huh?"

"Yup. Then you won't be so sad."

After dinner, holding Sarah's hand, we headed out to the barn. As we stepped inside, we heard Missy singing to the cows and their low moos in response, and we looked at each other and smiled. Then we entered the horses' stall and went to work, cleaning it out. We fed Big Red and Baby, and in the end, it was easy to see that Sarah was tired. It'd been a long day for her. I took her hand, and we walked back to the house. Betsy was waiting for us with a tub full of water for Sarah's bath.

Later, Betsy came to get me. "C'mon, we're having a meeting."

"Now?" I asked.

"Yes, we're all worried about you. We need to talk. You look like you died yourself."

We entered the office, and Lucy, Lester, Linda, and Missy sat there with worried expressions. "I'm okay. Just a little sad; that's all," I protested.

Lucy said, "We all know what mourning looks like, but there's something different this time. Why don't you tell us what's going on?"

My shoulders slumped. I had nothing positive to say, and I didn't want to burden them with my dark thoughts.

"For heaven's sake, Tiff, you don't need to shield us from your thoughts. We're all in this together, remember?" Betsy urged. "So spill."

I reminded myself that I was no longer the people pleaser I used to be, and I had the right to express myself without worrying about what others might think.

"Give her time, Betsy," prodded Missy.

I lifted my head and took in a deep breath before I began. I felt my emotions push to the top, and I shouted out. "I'm just so fucking angry. Angry at everything! How could God let that happen? How does he let someone like that bastard Blackie get rich by selling girls and then killing Brenda?" I hesitated, then sputtered, "Or any man for doing that? It's not fair! It's not fucking fair."

No one said anything. I continued in an exhausted whine, "Why do I get to live, and Brenda is the one to die? I'm don't deserve to live any more than she did; yet, she's the one dead," I asked.

"Ahh," said Lester. "Now we're getting somewhere."

There it was. My guilt for being alive while Brenda's life had been snuffed out. My guilt for living a beautiful life while so many didn't. Why had Lucy and Lester even chosen me, anyway?

Lucy and the girls looked at each other, relief written on their faces. I was talking about the "elephant" in the room, which appeared now and then. That wasn't the first time that one of us angels needed assurance that it was okay that things had worked out for us and not others. As I reviewed my outburst in my mind, my face burned with embarrassment. After all, I was the counselor and should know how to work out my feelings, shouldn't I?

Lucy, always tender, came to me and kissed the top of my bent head. "We love you, Tiff. You're hurting right now because you're a good person and care about what happens to others. The only thing we all can do is move forward to do what we can each day to make the world a better place."

Missy, Betsy, and Linda nodded in agreement. Lucy continued, "Lester and I have been giving some thought about you girls and the pressure you're under at times by carrying out our wishes … and perhaps losing a sense of yourself in doing so. Here is one of the ways we thought might help you become more aware of who we see you as—as an individual and what talent you bring to the group. Lucy smiled at Lester and reached for the cards he held out in his hand.

Lester interjected. "We know that sometimes it's easy for you to forget that you were very carefully chosen by us to be one of our angels. And yes, Linda, we *chose* you even though you're not always sure about that," he chuckled. "We want you to know that we honor each of you and thank you for helping us in our mission."

Lucy handed us each a card. "Starting with you, Missy, please read your card out loud so we can all hear you."

Missy, the sensitive one, opened her card, and her hands shook as she read in a soft voice. "You are our Angel of Healing and Regeneration. All those whom you come in contact with feel empowered by you to know that the Universe loves them."

We were mesmerized by what Missy had imparted, for it rang true for her. Next came Betsy.

Betsy, the realistic one, opened her card, and in a clear voice, read, "You are our Angel of Safety and Protection. All those whom you come in contact with walk taller feeling empowered by you to face life ahead without fear."

We looked at each other and smiled. Lucy and Lester had tagged Betsy's spirit for sure.

Linda, the rebel, was next. She opened her card and, with a rare shyness, read, "You are our Angel of Freedom. All those whom you come in contact with feel empowered by you to realize their inner strength to be free of anything restraining them from having or doing what they want."

We looked at Linda with an appreciation of what we knew to be true.

I opened my card and, in a shaky voice, read, "You are our Angel of Light and Transformation. All those whom you come in contact with feel empowered to believe and know that they are worthy of all the good that life has to offer."

We sat stunned with Lucy and Lester's consideration for each of us. There was complete silence as we felt the blessings of being together with a single goal of helping women from the streets into a better life. We shed tears, and I was more determined than ever to help shut down the pimps and johns that were controlling the streets.

Each of us felt a renewal in knowing what we stood for in the eyes of Lucy and Lester. We said goodnight to them with lightened hearts and a greater sense and determination of purpose. I felt blessed beyond words to be surrounded by Lucy and Lester and the other angels in my life. I couldn't allow doubt of where I was in life to be bumped by situations out of my control. I breathed in a sigh of contentment I hadn't felt in a long time.

We angels hugged each other goodnight with a greater appreciation of how we fit together to be the chosen ones. Scout nosed me, and I let him out for his final squirt of the day and then headed upstairs with him close behind.

CHAPTER 35

I overslept. I woke up to the dogs barking, the cows mooing, and the hens cackling. It seemed we had a visitor. Scout had already abdicated his throne at the foot of the bed and was nowhere to be seen. I crawled out of bed and went out onto the deck to see who had arrived. The vet was standing there, probably to check on Scout. I threw on some clothes and went downstairs to see.

After being only the three of us for many days, it now felt like a madhouse with everyone standing around the vet in the kitchen, watching him check out Scout. Only after he proclaimed Scout to be in perfect health did we all breathe a sigh of relief. The vet turned to Missy to explain what he wanted her to do if there were any signs of infection, and he wore an odd expression. Missy was beautiful and petite, appearing much more fragile than she was. Many a man had tried to win her heart but hadn't so far. I'd bet that the vet wouldn't score with her either since Missy seemed oblivious to his interest in her.

I put my arm around Sarah and kissed her. My cell phone rang, and I saw that it was Sam. I removed myself from Sarah and stepped outside. I was more myself and energetic than yesterday, so I answered brightly, "Good morning, Sam."

"I'm just checking to see when you'll be able to come to the station to answer some questions. Also, do you need me to pick you up?"

"I should be able to make it there by 11 o'clock. Does that work for you?"

"Sounds good. Do you ..."

"I'll drive myself, thank you." I interrupted.

"Okay, then. See you at 11."

"Bye."

"Where are you going?" whined Sarah with her nose pressed against the screen, staring out at me.

I'd forgotten big little ears hear all. "Down to the police station. When I get back, do you want to take a ride with me on Big Red?"

"Yesss!" she shouted, jumping up and down.

"Ask your mother first, though, remember?"

"Okay, Auntie Tiff, I will."

As I drove to the police station, I was torn between seeing Sam and dreading the review of the details of Brenda's attempted escape. When I arrived there, I was immediately ushered into the small room where I'd been before. And again, it was Sam's partner who greeted me.

"Hi, Tiffany. How ya doing?" she asked in a soft voice.

"Hi, Shirley. I'm fine. Thanks for asking."

Sam came into the room, and, once again, Shirley seemed curious to see how he would interact with me. I wondered if she fancied him. I glanced at her ring finger, and it was bare.

"I'm going to record our conversation. Shirley and I will ask some general questions. Are you okay doing this without an attorney?" asked Sam.

I nodded.

"Would you please say that out loud so we can record it?"

"Yes, I agree to speak with you without an attorney."

"Good. So let's begin."

They asked the typical questions – Why had I been with her? What was my relationship with her? How long had I known her? Was she my client? How long had I known Blackie? When did I first notice him at the airport? What direction had he come from? Did he have his gun in hand? How did I know he was after Brenda? Did I see him pull the trigger? Etc.

We went over and over every little detail, and it seemed to go on and on. Then Sam asked me, "Was it you who gave Brenda the money and gift cards found in her pocket?"

I nodded.

"Do you always help your clients out that way?"

"Not always, but when I can."

"You need to be careful with that, Tiffany. If word gets out, you'll have people come hunting you down for cash, and you don't want that to happen, believe me."

"I know," I replied in a small voice.

"Do you have an alarm system installed at your house?"

"Yes, an older one."

"I think I'd better check that out. You may want to upgrade to a better system," Sam said.

Shirley shifted in her seat, drawing our attention. "I can call my friend at ADT to take a look if you want."

"Let me check it out first," ordered Sam. "Then, you can have Shirley contact her friend if you want, Tiffany."

"Are we done yet?" I asked.

Shirley and Sam looked at each other and nodded. "Okay, for now. We may need to ask you more questions later," said Shirley.

I rose and stumbled out, exhausted. I couldn't wait to get back to the ranch and ride Big Red. That would bring me peace as nothing else could.

"Wait, Tiffany! I'll walk you out," said Sam, hurrying behind me.

When he reached my side, he put his arm around my shoulder. "You did well. I know it was difficult for you. How about we talk later, and I'll set up that target practice we talked about?"

"Sure, why not?" I agreed listlessly.

"Good. I also want to check out your alarm system. You're not staying at your house tonight, are you?"

"No, I'll be with my friends."

Shirley called out, "Sam, you've got a phone call. You need to grab it."

He squeezed my shoulder with affection. "Later."

CHAPTER 36

I arrived home to find Sarah waiting for me. She had her cowboy boots on and her denim shorts long enough to hit the tops of her boots. Sarah looked adorable with her long natural curly dark brown hair and hazel eyes that shone with joy. She lifted my heart. "Auntie Tiff! I'm ready!"

Betsy came forward. "You look like you've been through the wringer. Your ride will do you good. C'mon, I'll help saddle Big Red for you."

As we walked to the barn, Sarah ran ahead, and Betsy draped her arm around my waist. "Are you okay?"

I nodded. "Thanks. I'm glad you're back. I missed you." I paused, then added, "Do you miss being with your sister?"

Her brow wrinkled. "I love her because she's my sister. But it's you angels who are my real sisters if you know what I mean."

"Yeah, I do. I feel the same. No one can take the place of any of you."

Betsy lifted Sarah, so it was easier for me to hoist her up onto Big Red. I fit her in front of me, and she squealed with joy. "Bye, Mommy. We'll be back later."

"Okay, have a good ride," she said and waved. "You two go on. I'll keep Scout here."

We started slowly to give us time to accustom ourselves to riding together, and then we took off at a run. Our hair was pulled back by the breeze we created, and we both laughed with the sense of freedom that riding gave us. My worries flew past me, and with each minute, I felt like my old self again. We headed for my favorite spot, and my heart thudded with contentment. I clutched Sarah tighter to me as Big Red found his footing to climb the hill, and I became overwhelmed with tenderness toward her. I swallowed my emotion as I urged Big Red forward.

When we reached the spot, I was surprised to see that Rick was there. I had no idea he was back from the East coast. He smiled at me as he took in Sarah. We got down off Big Red and went to where he was sitting. Then Sarah raced back to get water from the saddlebag, and Rick turned to me, "Is she yours?"

I was taken aback at his question. It didn't sound pleasant the way he asked it. "Yup," I said, and waited to see what he'd say.

"Auntie Tiff, do you want a bottle of water too?"

Rick lifted his brow and smiled at that. I ignored him. "C'mon darling. Let's rest a bit before we head back," I called to Sarah.

"Okay," she answered.

"Rick, do you know if Ben shot the coyote? We haven't seen him around lately."

"Ben said he thought he wounded him, but the coyote ran off, and he couldn't find him to put him away for good."

"Gosh, that's not good news for any of us–especially the coyote."

"I wouldn't lose sleep over it. It's just a no-good coyote," Rick said with disgust.

I held back from snapping at him. "Still ..."

Sarah pulled on my sleeve. "He looks like Sue-Ling," she whispered.

"Yes, he does," I answered.

"Who's that?" asked Rick.

"Someone we know is all," I said.

Rick looked at me with expectation. "So have you thought it over? Are you gonna join me for dinner?"

I shook my head. "I'm afraid not. I'm not interested in dating anybody at this time."

Sarah studied me and was quiet. She pulled on me. "Can we go, Auntie Tiff?"

I rose. "Sure, we'd better go if we want to get in a long ride before it gets to be too late. Bye, Rick. Be sure and say hi to your dad, okay?"

He nodded and rose, dusting off his pants. "Will do." He lifted Sarah and helped to set her atop Big Red.

"Thanks, Rick."

He slapped Big Red on the butt and said, "See ya."

Big Red picked her way down the hill, and once on level ground, I nudged her to let loose. Sarah yelled, "Yahoo!" and we were off.

Sarah and I got into the rhythm of the horse's hoofs meeting the ground, and the music it made was pure heaven since we both loved to ride at top speed. My mind wandered back to what Betsy had said about no one taking the place of any of us angels. And it certainly was true for me. I knew our friendship was special because we didn't bicker as some sisters did. Perhaps it was because we'd been through so much ourselves that there was no need to create any more unrest and unhappiness. Been there, done that sort of thing. Perhaps, it was merely that we had grown enough spiritually to know we each had our own journey, and no one was better than the other. No matter what, I knew it was unusual to live as peacefully as we did, and I was grateful for it.

CHAPTER 37

I'd promised Sam that today was the day I'd go to target practice with him. I wasn't looking forward to it. I didn't like guns even though I'd spontaneously snatched the gun away from one of my clients when he'd passed out—more to protect myself rather than a souvenir of a horrendous experience. It was a reminder to me to be more careful whom I chose as a sex partner. A shudder came over me with the thought of that night.

I dressed plainly in jeans and a tee-shirt and left my hair loose. Then I pulled on my cowboy boots and clomped downstairs to help Missy with the animals. Ever since I'd taken over their care for the few days while she was away, I realized that it was unfair to expect her to do it all. Even though she said she didn't mind, it was a great feeling to care for Big Red and Baby myself at the times I was at the ranch.

Once in the barn, I smiled as I heard Missy singing. "Good morning, sunshine!" I called to her.

She turned and smiled. "Good morning, yourself. I'm glad to see you smiling."

"Yeah, me too."

"Where are you off to?" she asked.

"I told Sam I'd meet him for target practice. Despite not liking guns, I feel safer with it around. Go figure."

"Well, it's the only way to get your gun back, and you never know when you might need it."

"Right you are. Do you need anything in town as long as I'm heading in?"

"No, thanks. Betsy and I are heading up the road to Utah to get some groceries, so I think we're all set."

"Okay, then. I'll tend to the horses, and then I'll head out."

"Sounds good. See you later."

***

I pulled into the shooting range beside the police station and hopped out of the car. I headed in and walked to where Sam was standing in front of the counter. He was reaching for two pairs of headsets that were being handed to him. I was glad to see my gun resting on the shelf. When he saw me, he smiled broadly and waved me over. "Hi, there! Meet Joe," he said, bobbing his head toward the older man behind the counter.

I stretched my hand out so Joe could grasp it across the ample counter. Sam watched me with an approving look, and I realized that it'd been a long time since I'd even cared to see that appraising look from any man. It made me feel awkward, and I reached for the gun on the counter to draw attention away from myself.

"This way," Sam said as he headed toward the indoor shooting area.

I followed behind him, and I was glad to see that we were the only ones there. There were about ten cubicles in a row. Each was open in the front with targets in the background a reasonable distance away. There was a pulley overhead where paper mannequins could be attached, and the distance away from the shooter could be adjusted. On each side of the cubicle was bulletproof glass as protection against the shooter next door. Each space was large enough for two people to fit, but only one person was allowed to shoot at a time.

"We'll use this one," Sam said as he ushered me in. He put the headsets on the shelf where the shooter could use it to steady his position, or for personal items, or more massive machine guns and other weaponry.

"Wow, this is some setup," I said, trying to calm my nerves.

"C' mere, so I can help adjust your headset."

I shyly moved closer. Sam concentrated on pushing my hair back and adjusting my headset. He was close enough that I felt his body heat and took in his woodsy scent that was pleasing. After he finished, he raised my chin with his fist and smiled at me with searching eyes. My face heated, and I looked away. "Thanks, Sam."

Not to be deterred, he put his arm around me, turning me toward the front of the cubicle. He handed me my gun and pushed a box of bullets toward me. My hands shook as I slid in one bullet after another until there was 17 total in the magazine of my Glock. Sam put on his headset, and he stood close behind me to help me with the correct stance. He squeezed my shoulder, signaling me the okay to shoot. I aimed and fired. The gun recoiled, making me step back. I was surprised at the sound the weapon made because it wasn't as I imagined—it was a loud cracking sound. I turned to Sam in surprise.

He laughed. "It's not like anything else, is it?" I nodded in agreement. "Go ahead, shoot some more, so you get the feel of your gun."

I shot again and again and again. Each time I did, a feeling of power overcame me, and I knew I was in trouble. I liked firing the gun, and my shots were accurate enough that Sam said I was a natural. Anger rose from me as I thought about Brenda. I imagined Blackie, Johnny Wong, and all the rest of the men who used women to their advantage standing before me. If they'd been standing there, I would've shot them. And that scared me.

Sam watched me with a weird expression on his face. "I think you've had enough, Tiffany. I think it's time to stop."

"No, just a few more shots."

He shook his head and placed his hand on my arm. "You're getting into this too much."

"Okay, I'll stop," I said, knowing he spoke the truth.

"You had the same look on your face that I saw on too many faces of the soldiers I was with overseas. You're still angry over Brenda's death, aren't you?"

"Yeah, I am. I'll work it out, though. Don't worry."

"I'm sure you will. Should I keep the gun for you, or are you going to be okay having it with you?"

"I'd like it back, please."

"Okay, then. How about a cup of coffee before I go on duty?"

"My treat since you bought dinner the other night," I said.

While we sat sipping our coffee, Sam frowned. "You know, Tiffany, you still need to be careful. We believe that Lulu's, the Asian man's, and possibly Brenda's murder are all tied together somehow. And the thing that ties the three of them together is you. I'm worried. I hope wherever it is you're staying is safe."

"As safe as any place can be," I assured him.

"I still want to hear from you every night and morning, though," he demanded.

"Why do you need me to?"

"Because I care," he answered with pink cheeks.

257

"You know what I am, Sam—a girl from the streets. Why would you care?"

He looked annoyed. "I'm disappointed. I thought by now that you wouldn't allow some mistakes of the past to define you. Or do you like to play that up? Is that supposed to excite me?" he asked, his anger palpable.

"Don't you dare; you know better than that!" I sputtered.

"Do I? Whenever I try to get close, you immediately wrap your protective armor around you, and no one is allowed in—much less me."

"Well, I …."

"Never mind. It doesn't matter," Sam said as he rose from his seat. "I've got to run, or I'm going to be late. Thanks for the coffee." He hurried out, leaving me speechless.

I got up and paid the check with burning cheeks and drove back to the ranch.

CHAPTER 38

It was early morning and still dark outside when Missy climbed the stairs to tell me she'd received a telephone call from the rehab where Sue-Ling was staying. She'd gone missing, and they didn't know whether she'd left on her own accord or if Johnny Wong had taken her. We decided to let the others sleep in, and we'd tell them at breakfast. Sue-Ling was a problem; there was no doubt about it. I wondered if she'd try to come back to the ranch. I sure hoped she didn't.

At breakfast, it was Betsy who was the one most worried and angry. "Now, what do we do? It's not like we can put out an ABP alert or anything for her."

"No, but what we can do is try calling her. Maybe we can locate her that way," said Linda. "Have you already tried, Missy?"

Missy and I looked at each other, surprised we hadn't thought of that. "No, but I'll do it right now," she said as she searched for and found Sue-Ling's number on her phone.

"Wait!" hollered Linda. "Maybe we should only use a throwaway phone, so the call can't be traced back to us. You never know."

"Too late," said Missy. We stared at her and held our breath to see if Sue-Ling would answer. Missy shook her head. "Nothing."

"Give me her number, and I'll see if I can track it," offered Jerome.

"That'd be great," I said.

"I thought I'd let you all know that I've been called into the FBI to meet with them this afternoon at 3 o'clock. Wish me luck," Jerome said.

We all groaned. "What do you think will happen?" asked Betsy.

"I don't know. I heard that someone leaked some insider information, but it wasn't me. I also found out that I wasn't the only one they put on a temporary leave of absence."

"They'll clear you of any wrongdoing; I know they will," Linda said with conviction.

"We'll see," he replied, not too concerned.

Whether or not Jerome was allowed back to work at the FBI didn't necessarily change the dynamics of having him living at the house with us. Once something gets established, it's challenging to go back to the way things were before. Especially now, with his growing relationship with Linda. We angels had become so close that not one of us had the desire to leave the ranch and the others. For Linda to remain as one of the angels, did that mean Jerome would have to be here as well?

I studied Jerome as he responded to Sarah about something she'd asked him. It was nice for her to have a male perspective on things—a better balance. If Jerome left, he'd leave a hole in all of us. I was pulled away from my thoughts by the ringing of my cell phone. It was Sam. I hadn't called him last night, and I wondered if he was still upset with me.

"Good morning, Sam," I said in a cool tone, still annoyed from his comment the day before.

"Tiffany, I'm calling to warn you. We picked up Johnny Wong late yesterday afternoon, but he escaped early this morning. You need to be on the lookout for him. Stay out of town, do you hear me?"

"How'd that happen?"

"It's a long story. You don't even want to know ..."

"But, I do ..."

"Oops, I've got to run. I'll call you later."

Everyone at the table turned my way, curious to know what'd happened. After I told them, they looked grim except for Sarah, who asked, "What's wrong?"

Never holding anything back from her, Betsy answered her honestly, "A dangerous man escaped from prison."

"Is he coming here?" she asked, innocently.

"We certainly hope not. But remember our rule about strangers. If you see any strangers around here, come to me or any of the others, understand?"

"Yes, Mommy."

"Good girl," I said. "I'm going to be using the office today. I have to conduct a few sessions over the phone. Everyone okay with that?"

All nodded, and I got up and headed that way. Oddly enough, many of the clients I'd been working with had reached the point where they didn't need me regularly. They'd be okay on their own for a while. I had their telephone numbers, and I'd call and check in with them. I'd also make my daily call to pick up any messages from my answering machine at the house. Until Johnny Wong was behind bars, I couldn't take a chance by going into town and being followed back to the ranch.

I sat at the desk, and instead of calling any clients, my mind wandered to Sam. He certainly had been angry with me after our target practice. I blushed at the thought of what he'd said. I knew clinging to my identity as a girl from the street was long overdue for me to dump it. I was a girl who *used* to be on the streets, true, but that's not who I was today. So what was that all about? Why couldn't I forgive myself entirely for what'd happened in the past? What was it going to take?

I heard the outside alarm buzz, and I joined the others in the Bat Room to see what the computers showed had set it off. We could barely make out something limping along, low to the ground. It was dragging itself forward, and it was evident that, whatever it was, was hurt. As it came closer and we got a better view of it, Betsy gasped. "I can't believe it! Is that our coyote?"

Betsy raced outside to where it had fallen in a heap beside the barn. The rest of us were not far behind. The dogs had run ahead and circled it, barking. I peered over Betsy's shoulder as she knelt over the body, and it was difficult not to cry out in anguish to see the Coyote's suffering. He looked starved, and his left hip was angled high, and his left leg was twisted with several bones showing. He lay there, panting in pain with pleading eyes. "Get my rifle," ordered Betsy.

"No!" argued Missy. "I can save him. Let me at least try."

"Please, Mommy!" pleaded Sarah. "Don't shoot him!"

"Let Missy try," I urged. "She'll know within 12 hours. Then the decision can be made to put him down if he doesn't improve. I'll call the vet to come."

"Let's move him into the barn," suggested Linda.

"Yes, we can put him in the birthing stall. He won't be able to get out from there," said Missy.

Linda ran to get the stretcher, and we worked together to pick him up and place him in the barn. He allowed Missy and Sarah to get near him but eyed Betsy as if he knew she'd do away with him if she had her way. Linda, Jerome, and I stood back and watched.

"What made him come here?" wondered Linda.

"Probably the idea of food," Betsy answered.

"Sometimes, if things become desperate enough for an animal, they'll seek out a place they instinctively know will be safe," said Missy.

The other three of us angels looked at each other knowingly. After all, Missy was the Angel of Healing and Regeneration. If anyone could help this poor coyote, she could.

The others left, and I stayed behind, wanting to watch. For a long time now, Sarah had told us she wanted to become a nurse when she grew up. Working beside Missy, there was no doubt that she'd be a good one—smart, loving, and kind.

Missy, with all her patience, was a loving teacher to Sarah, showing and explaining each of her moves. Since the coyote wanted nothing to do with the vet, he allowed Missy to continue to help him. The vet stood back with a tender look and watched Missy and Sarah work together, each assuring the coyote that he'd be well again soon.

"Here, Missy, take this syringe. This medicine will knock him out, and we'll see then what we can do to set his leg," the vet said.

At the prick of the needle, the coyote gave a weak yelp and closed his eyes. The vet moved Missy and Sarah aside and knelt beside the coyote. As Missy had done before, he now became the teacher, explaining everything he was doing. Soon, the worst was over, and all three rose and brushed off their pants.

Sarah came to me, smiling with pride. "He's going to be alright, isn't he, Auntie Tiff?"

"I think with your help, he's got a good chance," I said, pulling her into a tight hug.

Betsy joined us, and Sarah ran into her open arms, excited. "Thank you, Mommy, for not shooting him. He's going to be okay."

Betsy and I smiled as we overheard Missy say, "I don't think that's necessary for you to come every day. I can call you if something changes. That way, you won't be wasting your time."

The look on the vet's face was amusing. It was apparent that Missy wasn't aware that his interest was in her, not the coyote. "We'll see," he responded as he picked up his bag and headed out.

Missy walked toward us. "Sarah, we're going to let the coyote sleep now. He'll be out for a long time, so we'll come back later to check on him."

CHAPTER 39

The next few days were peaceful. Missy and Sarah spent a lot of time pampering the coyote. Although still skittish, he eagerly awaited their visits and his treats of fresh meat. The coyote seemed to get better each day, which made Missy and Sarah ecstatic. The vet had been here twice so far, despite Missy's insistence that he didn't need to come.

Betsy was involved with an online course about investments. She wanted to learn all about indexing, although she said only a fool would get thoroughly involved with that.

Jerome had his job back, so he was in good standing with the FBI. They had arrested someone relatively new to the FBI who'd been caught giving away secret information. Jerome was still with us staying in the shed at night, and we were all happy he was, especially Linda. She was continually on the hunt to see if anything else was going on regarding human trafficking over the web.

As requested, I continued my calls with Sam, which gave us a way to get to know each other better. Things seemed to have quieted down for him as well. They hadn't been able to track down Johnny Wong, but no doubt, it was only a matter of time before he showed his face again. Sam thought he might have gone to Los Angeles until things cooled down.

We had received no word regarding Sue-Ling, and we had no idea where she was or what'd happened. I felt sure she'd contact us again because we'd provided her a safe place. But so far, that hadn't happened.

To keep me busy, I made strawberry jam, which turned out to be fun, and each day, I mucked out Big Red's stall and rode her. But the truth was, I was bored without my usual city schedule. I'd bought bullets when I was at target practice with Sam, so that morning, I decided to set up target practice outside— more for something to do than anything else. Without him beside me, it wasn't as exciting as the first day of shooting, but I took my time and trained for accuracy. I think Sam was right when he said I had a natural ability because I was pretty good.

As I stood ready to shoot another round, I felt my cell phone buzzing in the back pocket of my jeans. I reached for it and saw it was a number I didn't recognize. Usually, I'd let the call go to voicemail so

I wouldn't have to deal with another robocall, but something urged me to answer it instead.

"Hello?" I heard only background noise.

"Hello?" Still no answer.

I knew better than to ask if it were Sue-Ling in case it was Johnny Wong. I'd learned my lesson the hard way a few years back. I was ready to end the call when I barely heard, "Tiffany? I need your help."

"Who's this?"

"It's me… Sue-Ling."

"Sue-Ling, where are you?" I heard muffling sounds.

"In Utah."

"Is Johnny Wong with you?" I asked, goosebumps spreading across my body.

"No, of course not," she answered quickly. Too quickly.

Something wasn't right. "Where are you in Utah?"

"I'm at the casino."

"Which one, Sue-Ling?" I asked impatiently.

"Cowboy's Heaven."

"My God! That's not far from Vegas! How did you get there?"

More muffling, and then she whined, "Can you come and get me or not?"

Her story was too rehearsed, and I smelled a rat. "Is this number a good one to call you back?"

"Call me back? When?"

"In about 20 minutes or so. Do you have somewhere safe to stay until I can get there?"

"At the casino."

"Okay, hang in there, and I'll call you back at this number as soon as I can, Sue-Ling."

"Okay."

"Goodbye, Sue-Ling."

I gathered the girls together. "We have a problem." As I explained the situation, Linda, Betsy, and Missy looked alarmed.

"Sue-Ling called for you to pick her up in Utah? Does she think she's coming back here?" asked Linda. "I don't think that's such a good idea, do you?"

"Me, either," seconded Betsy. "We don't know why she left the rehab where she was, or if she left it on her own. I think that by going there for her, you'll be heading into nothing but trouble. I don't think you should go there at all."

"Missy? What do you think?" I asked, knowing she'd want to save her somehow.

"I think we should work it through the rehab where she'd been staying," she answered, surprising us all. "Maybe they could send the police to pick her up."

"Yes," answered Betsy. "But we can't force her to go back into rehab if she doesn't want to. I'm not sure they'll even take her back, or there'll be a bed available for her. I had to do a lot of talking to get her in there in the first place."

"So what do we do about Sue-Ling?" asked Linda. "Would Sam be able to help us out? Why don't you call him, Tiff?'

"Do we want him to find out what we've been up to? He's the police, after all." I was quiet. "I suppose I could tell him that one of my clients called for help, and since Johnny Wong is her pimp, I think they might be together, wanting to trap me."

"That might work," said Betsy.

"You do realize, don't you, that Sue-Ling could burst this place wide open. There's no guarantee that she'll keep quiet. I don't think her word is good for that, but I could be wrong. Are we willing to take the chance?" I asked, then added, "We'll need Lucy and Lester's blessing no matter what we decide to do."

We gathered around the house phone and put it on speaker so we all could take part in the conversation. We were lucky that Lester was already home from the soup kitchen and there with Lucy.

Betsy explained the situation. "So what do you think, Lester and Lucy? Should we bring Sam in on this? You know if we do, it may be the end of privacy for the ranch."

I could picture the two of them shaking their heads as they each debated within themselves what to do. Lucy finally answered, "We can't leave Sue-Ling without help. I had a good feeling about Sam when I met him at the airport that day. Do we have a choice?"

"This is all my fault," bemoaned Lester.

In a placating tone, Lucy said, "You're talking about spilled milk, Lester. Don't go down that path."

I piped up. "I'm only willing to bring Sam into this on my terms. I want to keep this quiet and out of the

271

papers, and I think we can do that if it's just the two of us. I'm not sure about what's going on with Sue-Ling, and I'm not positive that Johnny Wong is with her. It's just a feeling I have, although I've learned to trust them."

Missy asked, "What do we do with Sue-Ling if we get her back?"

"Good question, Missy," said Linda. "What *do* we do with her?"

We all were silent for several moments until Lucy spoke up, "Bring her back here to our house. She can stay with us until we can move her on. That shouldn't be more than 24 hours."

"I'll make some calls to see if there's room for her elsewhere," Lester said. "We need to work through an agency that is better equipped to handle her."

"Are you sure you want to take her on until then?" asked Betsy.

"Yes," chorused Lucy and Lester. "Why not give Sam a call then, Tiff, and see what you can work out with him," said Lester. "We'll wait to hear from you."

CHAPTER 40

I went into the office for privacy and nervously put in my call to Sam. It rang and rang, and I thought he wasn't going to answer. Then, at last, I heard his breathless, "Hey, Tiffany. Whew! I'm out of breath. It's my day off, and I was outside in the garden."

His day off? Perfect! "I'm pretty sure I know where Johnny Wong is."

"How do you know that?" he asked, surprised.

"I received a call from one of my clients, and he's her pimp. She wants me to meet her, and I think he's there with her, waiting to trap me."

"Where are they?"

"I'm not going to tell you."

"Why not?" he asked, completely baffled.

"I'd rather show you."

"Tiffany, why don't you let me call it in and let the police handle it instead of us?"

"I have my reasons. Do you trust me, Sam? Trust me enough to take a short trip with me so I can meet my client and see if Johnny Wong is with her?"

"Tiffany, why not involve the police?"

"I don't trust the police, Sam. But I do trust you."

He hesitated, and I knew that he was mulling over what I'd said. "I don't like this, Tiffany, but okay, I'll do it."

We decided to meet out on Route 15 by the speedway in thirty minutes. I called the girls into the office and told them what I'd arranged. Next, I dialed Lucy and Lester to fill them in, and finally, I called Sue-Ling to say to her I'd meet her in the lobby of the casino in 90 minutes or so. I'd call her again when I got close.

When I arrived at our designated spot to meet, Sam was already there. He stepped out of his car and pointed to an empty place where I could park. He'd decided he was going to drive, which was fine by me. Sam wore snug blue jeans and a simple black t-shirt which stretched across his broad chest. His arms were tanned and muscled, making him look toned and handsome. I blushed as he caught me looking him over.

I grabbed my large purse with my gun and a bottle of water inside and hopped out of the car. Then I locked it and jumped into Sam's car. "Which way?" he asked.

"Head North. Keep on Route 15 until I tell you when to turn off."

"Aye, aye, Captain," he smiled.

I returned the smile but said nothing.

"So tell me about this client of yours. What's her name?"

"Sue-Ling."

"Are you kidding? Sue-Ling is your client? Why didn't you say so?"

"Why would I have?"

"We believe she's involved in some bad stuff with Johnny Wong. How did you get mixed up with her?"

"Through friends."

"The same friends you've been staying with?"

I nodded. "Yes."

"Do your friends understand it's important to vet the people? What do they do, anyway?"

"They run the soup kitchen on Martin Luther King Boulevard," I answered with pride.

"Ahh, the Black Samaritans. I thought that was them when they came to pick you up at the airport after the shooting. Now it makes sense."

"How do you know about them?" I asked, curious.

"Do you realize how many people we pick up off the street for prostitution or drug dealing each day? Frankly, most of the worst cases are still alive because of that soup kitchen."

"Ohh."

"These are crazy times filled with stupid people who are only alive from overdoses because of the medication now available. That's enough to blow your mind."

"You sound upset," I said.

"Upset? I get so pissed off when I see these young kids still in Junior High or High School doing that shit. And I haven't even touched on the problem of human trafficking! Don't get me started on that."

I remained quiet and looked out the window at the dull desert landscape as we drove along. I felt Sam's hand on my knee and turned to face him. "I apologize. I'm sorry to rant like that. It's so frustrating to see how so many people in the other parts of the world have nothing while we in America have so much. Yet, we're willing to throw it all away for the pleasure of drugs and sex."

My face got hot, and I turned away.

"I'm not talking about you …"

But it was too late. Sam had already made his point. I sat stiffly in my seat, wishing for the miles to fly by so that we could get this over and done. I was beginning not to care whether we captured Johnny Wong or not. I just wanted to be back at the ranch and the comfort of my home. We both were quiet for a while until the oppressive atmosphere became unbearable.

"Let's plan this out, shall we?" Sam finally said.

I nodded in agreement. "So that you know, we're headed to Cowboy's Heaven. I told Sue-Ling I'd meet her in the lobby there."

"Smart move, Tiffany. Keep the meeting out in the open where safety comes about with numbers. Good thinking."

I knew Sam was trying to appease me, but I was having none it. "I told Sue-Ling I'd call her when I got closer. What do you have?"

"I think you should let me go in first by myself so I can check it out. I brought along a badge for you. I'll deputize you to keep everything on the up and up if you know what I mean."

"Do you always keep an extra badge around?" I asked. "Where do you keep it? In the glove compartment?"

When he blushed, I had my answer. "I have it in there for emergencies... you never know."

I smiled despite myself. It was evident that Sam liked to be prepared for anything. He probably had been an Eagle Scout when he was younger, I thought. When he saw me smile, he laughed. "I know. You don't have to say anything. I get teased about it all the time. They don't call me Ready Eddie for nothing."

I blushed furiously at his nickname. Did he realize what that name could mean? I burst out laughing. "I wouldn't admit that to everyone. They might get the wrong idea."

His face reddened. "Believe me, I know."

"Here! Turn off here," I ordered and drew in a deep breath as we headed toward the casino. My heart pounded with foreboding, and I wondered what mess I'd gotten us into this time.

CHAPTER 41

I sat in the car and watched Sam enter the casino. Once he spotted Sue-Ling or Johnny Wong, he'd slip into the men's room and call me. I closed my eyes and leaned back against the seat. In so many ways, I wished it would be just Sue-Ling we'd have to handle. In other ways, the thought of having Johnny Wong finally behind bars would be a relief.

Time passed. I waited and waited for Sam's call. I checked my phone several times to make sure it was on and held it in my hand to answer it quickly. Nothing.

After 35 minutes had passed, my stomach roiled at the thought that something had gone wrong. I got out of the car and made my way into the casino. Once inside, I stepped back against the wall of the lobby and tried not to look conspicuous while I looked around. I didn't see any of them—Sam, Sue-Ling, or Johnny Wong. I began to walk into the central part of the casino, where slot machines were scattered, and gambling tables sat with dealers behind them when I felt a tap on my shoulder. I quickly turned around and was shocked to see Johnny Wong. "What are you doing here?" I squealed.

"Shut up! You're coming with me now!"

"Let go of me right now or I'll scream," I protested.

"I wouldn't do that if you want your boyfriend alive," he threatened.

"What do you mean?" I asked, dread filling me.

"C'mon," he said as he pulled me with him and squeezed my wrist so tight that I winced. Then he put his other arm around my waist and pulled me close enough that it looked like we were a couple in a tight embrace.

"Where's Sue-Ling?" I whispered. "You haven't hurt her, have you?"

"Wouldn't you like to know," he teased with a malicious smile.

"Oh, my God! Where are you taking me?" I asked as he pushed me into the elevator.

"You'll see," he laughed mirthlessly.

Others approached, waiting to get inside with us, but Johnny stood with his back toward them, and his arms spread, blocking their entrance. As the elevator doors closed for good, he smiled at his success at keeping them away.

We rode to the top of the casino to the presidential suite. Johnny took out the room card and slid it down the magnetic holder for us to enter. He shoved me hard into the room, and I nearly fell. When I righted myself, I saw Sue-Ling lolling across the couch, her head hanging off it, out cold. At first, it looked as if she'd overdosed, and my heart nearly stopped, but then I heard a small sigh escape her lips. I saw a needle and white powder on the coffee table and cried out, "Why, Johnny? She loves you, and if you love her, why give her that shit?"

"Me? She doesn't love me. She's in love with cocaine," he announced in a harsh, hurt tone. "And she'll do anything to get it too."

I felt sick because I remembered when I'd done things I've since regretted—all for that high that only comes with cocaine.

"Where's Sam?" I asked, looking around for him.

He pushed me further into the room, and I saw him slumped against the wall in the furthest corner. He had fallen or had been forced there by Johnny. He was not moving, and I wondered if Johnny had drugged him. When I saw blood on Sam's head, I was relieved, believing he must have been knocked unconscious instead of being doped. As we moved closer to him, Johnny kicked at his prone body, and Sam moaned and struggled to sit up straight. He reached his hand up to touch the spot on his head where he was hurt. Then, he opened his eyes and seemed surprised and embarrassed to see me standing there.

Sam scrambled onto his feet and grabbed my hand to pull me to him, blocking Johnny's view of him. For that second of time, he startled me by winking. I watched Sam discreetly tuck his cell phone behind him before he stepped forward.

Johnny grabbed my other hand and jerked me back, twisting my arm. He removed his gun from his belt and held it to my head. "Stand back, dick head," he threatened Sam.

"Why are you doing this, Johnny?" I asked.

"Because I can," he laughed harshly.

"How did you find Sue-Ling?"

"She contacted me, said she couldn't live without me."

"Really?" I asked, curious. "Do you mean she couldn't live without you, or she couldn't live without the drugs?"

He jerked me, tightening his grip on my twisted arm, making me squeal in pain and tears to form. "You think I don't know who you are, bitch? I know where you come from, and you're no better than Sue-Ling or any of the other whores from the street."

"Leave her alone," Sam ordered, "and put the gun down."

"It's payback time. Tiffany's coming with me. She'll bring me a pretty penny, and there's nothing you can do about it, loser."

Johnny took the gun away from my head and pointed it at Sam.

"No!" I shouted. "I'll go with you. Just don't shoot him."

"I can't promise that now, can I?"

"What about Sue-Ling? You're not leaving her behind, are you?" I asked, trying to divert attention away from Sam.

"She's too much trouble."

"Let me grab my purse," I pleaded as Johnny began to pull me with him to get closer to Sam. I twisted away from Johnny and bent down to pick up my purse from where I'd dropped it on the floor when he'd grabbed my arm. Then, in one smooth move, I lifted my bag and swung it at Johnny's head. The weight of the gun in my purse knocked him backward, and his weapon went off, hitting the ceiling above us. Sam lurched forward and tackled him, pinning him to the floor.

I reached for Johnny's gun and held it in my hands and felt the power it gave me. I looked at Sam, who wore a funny expression as he watched me.

"Grab the handcuffs from my back pocket, Tiffany, and give them to me," he ordered.

I did as I was asked and looked on as Johnny squirmed on the floor and yelled obscene words and epitaphs. "Here," I said to Sam, handing him the bandana I'd thrown into my purse at the last minute. "That'll shut him up."

With shaking hands, I put the gun down on the coffee table, relieved to lay it aside.

"Are you alright, Tiffany?" asked Sam, concerned as he saw me rubbing my shoulder.

"Better than you. It looks as if you are going to need a stitch or two."

We heard sirens in the background, and Sam pulled out his phone and punched in a number. "Up here, in the penthouse."

"Who was that?" I asked, wondering who he'd called.

His face flushed. "My partner, Shirley. I wasn't going to go rogue against police policy. I had her follow us in case we needed help, especially if we ran into Johnny Wong. While Johnny went to find you, I called her and told her we'd need an ambulance for Sue-Ling. She fought him pretty hard because she didn't want the drugs."

My heart lifted. "Really? She didn't want them?"

Sam shook his head. I couldn't wait to tell the girls that bit of good news. So Johnny had kidnapped her, then. Good. Another charge could be placed against him to give him a longer jail sentence.

I called Lucy and Lester. When they heard what'd happened, they asked Sam if the ambulance could take Sue-Ling back to Las Vegas. They'd pay extra for the trip because they wanted her close enough for them to visit her so she wouldn't be alone. I think Sam was amazed that they'd be willing to pay the extra money and surprised they could afford to do that. Lucy said she'd let the girls know what'd happened because I couldn't call them myself since Sam was with me.

Sam refused to go to the local hospital, and at his insistence, the medics cleaned and stitched him up right then and there. He wore a big bandage on his head, and Shirley went to his side to tease him. "Hey, buddy, it looks like you got the short end of the stick."

They both laughed, and then Shirley led Johnny Wong down the backstairs with the gag still on so he'd make as little a commotion as possible. The same policeman, who'd been there at the time my car had received its written warning message, was with her.

After everyone had vacated the penthouse, and we settled up with the casino, I took one look at Sam, who was trying to keep his eyes open. The medic had given him something for the pain. "C'mon, I'll drive us back."

He studied me, and I knew he had something on his mind. Instead, he nodded and said, "Okay, deal."

CHAPTER 42

A few days later, I found myself once again driving into the city to meet with the police to file a report—this time against Johnny Wong. Sam had chosen to do the right thing by alerting his partner to what we were up to, but it stung a bit to see that the local newspaper had picked up the story. Luckily, they'd kept me out of it, but it meant that Sue-Ling would need a lawyer to clear up some of her past happenings.

It would be a while before anything would get resolved, and during that time, Johnny Wong would remain in prison—a relief to all. Because of the newspaper article highlighting human trafficking, prostitution, and addiction, I had several new clients. I decided to move back to my house the following day and get my business in order.

When I arrived at the police station, I walked in and headed back toward Sam's office. I startled him when I entered his office without warning. He sat at his desk, pouring over the photos of the recent murders. My having had contact with the victims linked me to them. When Sam saw me, he smiled broadly. "C'mon in, Tiffany. How are you doing?"

"I'm okay. How's your head? I see the bandage is gone."

"Yeah, I was tired of being teased about it."

"I don't blame you," I said. Sighing loudly, I plopped myself down in the only chair available.

"What's the matter?" he asked.

"I guess I'm just tired of the whole situation. Too many murders, for what? Power over another human being? Money? Sex? Drugs? What?"

"All of the above, to be honest." He cleared his throat. "Listen, I want to talk to you about something if you're up for it."

"Okay, I guess. What is it?"

He studied me. "Are you aware that when you hold a gun in your hand, it changes your whole demeanor? Do you know what I'm talking about?"

Immediately, my face heated because I knew what he'd said was true.

"I know what you're feeling. I experienced the same thing when I was assigned to special ops in the army. I felt so powerful with a gun in my hand, and my whole attitude changed. I became someone I'm not inside. I was a bully all during training. I believed I could rule the world, and to hell with anyone who got in my way." He paused to let me take in what he'd said. "That's what I read on your face when we were at target practice, and again when you picked up Johnny's gun before you handed it to me."

I blushed even more. "You're not that way now. So what happened to change you?" I asked, curious.

He hesitated, embarrassed. "I saw what it was like to kill someone—someone not much different than me. It sickened me."

"You spent three years in Afghanistan, and you even earned medals. How did you get through it if you didn't want to kill others?"

"I needed to protect my men. They had to come first—not an easy choice."

"So that's it then? Change from being the bully to become the protector?"

"Yes and no. When you know you have power without a gun, you no longer desire it, and you only use it when it's necessary."

"Why are you telling me this, Sam?" I asked, confused.

He looked at me with a steady stare. "Find your power without the gun, Tiffany," he ordered. "It's a nice space to be in, trust me."

Shirley stopped in the doorway, cutting off our conversation. She looked from Sam to me with a raised eyebrow. "Hi there, Tiffany. Ready to sign some paperwork?"

***

Earlier, the girls had asked to meet with me in the office that night. Jerome would watch Sarah, who'd been clinging to me ever since she'd overheard that I could've been killed when I met up with Johnny Wong. Even though we all tried to make light of it, she'd taken it to heart for the first few days, and only now was ready to release that fear. It hurt that I'd caused her any anguish.

I was quiet as we angels sat together to discuss Sue-Ling and talk about the other new girls that would be coming to us soon. It was unusual that we didn't already have a new girl with us now.

Later, Betsy asked, "Tiffany, would you feel safer staying here?"

I looked up in confusion. "What do you mean?"

"Live here permanently. After all, you're becoming known for helping girls who want to get out of the business and away from their pimps. Is it safe for you to be alone in town?"

"Would you like me to come and stay with you for a few days?" intercepted Linda.

"No, but thanks anyway. I'm going to be perfectly fine, and I'll still be back here on the weekends as usual." I became lost in thought.

"Everything okay?" said Missy.

I blushed. "I had an interesting conversation with Sam; that's got me thinking about things…"

"Oh, I want to hear all about it," urged Linda, excited to think it had something to do with romance.

"Me, too," added Missy with a smile.

"So spill!" said Betsy.

After I'd told them what Sam had said about me finding my power, they nodded their heads in agreement.

"Sounds like good advice," said Linda.

"What makes you feel empowered?" I asked her.

She answered in a slow, thoughtful way. "My skills as a computer coder give me the power to protect some of the victims of human trafficking and other horrendous acts of violence." She looked at us and grimaced. "But I didn't learn I had that power until I took action against the very thing I despised. And that was only after what happened to my girlfriend."

We nodded, knowing that'd been the impetus for her raid on the bad guys.

"What about you, Betsy?" I asked.

"Me? Well, I guess I feel empowered when I use men to get what I want." At the expressions on our faces, she added, "It's not pretty, I know. But after feeling that I had *no* power what with any man in my family using me for his sexual pleasure, I learned how to make a man desire me so that he'd do anything to have sex with me. That was how I learned I *had* power, and I use it to get what I want. No man will ever have power over me again. I won't allow it."

"How are you going to guarantee that?" I asked.

"Simple," she said. "I'm done with men. I'm not getting involved with any man again."

"No surprise there," said Linda with a chuckle.

"What about you, Missy?" I asked. Linda, Betsy, and I leaned forward to hear her soft voice.

"I guess I'm a lot like Betsy in that I had zero power when I was little. It was only when the nurse in the hospital told me that she wasn't going to let me die and that the Universe had more in store for me that I began to want to live and learn what that something more was. The fact is I feel empowered each time I help to heal someone's injury; it's like I'm healing the pain in my soul for what happened to that lost little girl that no one cared for and loved."

Her sorrowful words brought tears to our eyes because we knew that although she now felt lucky to be alive, there were many points in her life where she was sorry she had been. "There are so many who need help..." she drifted off.

"So what about you, Tiff?" asked Betsy. "What's holding you back from feeling empowered?"

I stared at the three of them and searched for the words to express what I wanted to say. Finally, in exasperation, I said, "How can I feel empowered about anything if I can't even forgive myself for what I've done?"

"What's holding you back from doing that?" asked Linda, curious.

"All three of you have responded to circumstances beyond your control. Me? I've created my past circumstances with my own choices!"

"So what?" said Betsy, "No one is perfect, and we learn by our mistakes."

"I know that," I responded, grumpily. "But I've hurt so many people. And I'm a counselor? A fraud is what I am. If I can't get my own life under control, how can I truly help someone else?"

"Hold on!" cried Linda. "Betsy's right. You don't have to be perfect to help someone else. Besides, you're talking about what Lucy calls spilled milk, Tiff. You can't change the past."

"I realize that ..."

"Does this have something to do with your parents?" asked Missy.

I nodded. Missy was right. It had everything to do with them.

Betsy and the others got up and came to pat my shoulder, encouraging me to straighten that mess out. "Time for a group hug," said Betsy. We formed a circle for our group hug and chanted our mantra – "sisters together, sisters for life."

CHAPTER 43

In some aspects, it was hard for me to pack up the extra things I'd taken with me to the ranch and drive back to my house all alone. It'd be safe for me now to be there with both Johnny Wong and Blackie behind bars, but I'd miss the hustle and bustle of the ranch. As soon as I pulled into my driveway, any disparaging thoughts left me, and once again, I felt the pleasure I had each time I viewed my home as the accomplishment it was—a symbol of my hard work of turning my life around—albeit with the support of my friends.

When I tried to enter through the front door, I could barely open it. There was a massive pile of mail covering the floor. I scooped it up and noticed that along with the regular mail, there was a pretty pink envelope with a handwritten address in loopy writing. I placed the letter on the kitchen bar and pulled out the card. It was from my aunt whom I'd not spoken to in years, and I couldn't imagine how she'd found me or why she was writing to me. Inside there was a short note, "I thought you might be able to help. She's my neighbor's daughter. The last time my neighbor heard from her, she was in Las Vegas. Please do what you can. Much love, Aunt Dora." There was a newspaper clipping with a picture of the girl who looked as if she were no older than 18 or 19. At the very bottom of the note was a "P.S. Your parents send their love."

My eyes filled. At the start of my downward spiral, I didn't want anything to do with my parents. After a while, their calls dwindled and then ultimately stopped after I'd changed my cell phone number several times, making it impossible for them to reach me. That was the one thing I seemed unable to forgive myself. Who does that to parents who were kind to me? Who cared for me and only wanted my happiness? I thought of Sam, who'd give anything to have his parents still alive, and shame washed over me.

I plopped down in my favorite chair by the fireplace and read the article about the missing girl. It was the same story that happened to so many of us. We come here to Las Vegas to begin a new life only to get caught up in something else that turns out to be our undoing. The more I studied her picture, the more I had a fleeting memory of seeing her or someone like her at one of the casinos.

I debated about becoming involved in locating this missing girl. If I could find her and help her reunite with her parents, that might be a way for me to make up for my actions at the time I'd handled my situation so poorly with my parents. I knew I was grasping at straws, but I had to see what I could do.

My first new client wasn't due until the next day, which gave me plenty of time to ask the girls on the street if they'd seen the missing girl. Because the two pimps who'd been a threat to me were now behind bars, I no longer had to check in with Sam each morning and night. That gave me greater freedom to explore what I could find out about the missing girl.

I got up from my chair and began to finish unpacking the things I'd brought back from the ranch. Then, I went into the kitchen to check out the nearly empty refrigerator. I made a list of what I needed and hopped back into my car to head for the grocery store.

After restocking my refrigerator, I dressed into something more casual and headed out to the streets of old Las Vegas. Even though it was early for most of them to be out on the "stroll," I saw several prostitutes I recognized and approached them. I showed them the clipping of the young girl. "Have you seen this girl around?"

Not interested, two of them shook their heads with hardly a glance at the photo.

"How about you, Lucinda?" I asked the one I knew best.

"Here, let me see," she said as she reached for the clipping. She shook her head. "Sorry, I haven't. Pictures like this show a smiling, happy girl, but we both know that look doesn't stay long if you get caught in the shadow world, right?"

I nodded. I had to agree.

Next, I drove to the soup kitchen to see if anyone there had seen her. An old homeless woman yanked the clipping out of my hand. "I seen her... I seen her with a bunch of whores standing on a street corner near that casino down there."

The casino she was talking about was the same one that Lulu had frequented. So that made my decision easy to visit it that night.

Most solicitations are done now over the internet and social media. The interesting thing about what the homeless woman had said about seeing the missing girl on the street is that was how some of the pimps broke in their new girls—set them out walking the street known for its prostitution, called the "stroll."

Later, I slipped into a dress that made me look sexy but not overdone, and I applied very little makeup. I made my way into the same bar where I'd met with Lulu. I was early. I looked around and didn't see anyone I recognized, so I sat in the corner to observe all who entered or left the bar. Although business was not that busy, I knew it'd pick up in time.

About a half-hour later, I watched three young girls dressed to the teeth come in and sit at a round high-top table near the bar. At first, I couldn't decide whether they were tourists or local young girls toying with trouble. They weren't acting like most of the prostitutes I knew. After observing one of them approach a gentleman and point the other two out as a trio, I shook my head at my stupidity. Locals. I was pleasantly surprised to see the gentleman smile at what one of the girls said and turn away with a dismissive shake of his head. The girl shrugged her shoulder and mouthed "Bummer," to the other two girls and laughed.

I waited a few minutes before I approached them. "Howdy, what are you girls up to?"

"What's it to you?" snapped the least pretty one of the trio.

"Are you aware that you can get jail time for soliciting?"

"Whaddya mean?" the second girl asked.

"Don't say anything," ordered the first girl.

"I'm just warning you girls that you're heading for trouble big time. The last thing you girls need is to anger one of the pimps because you're cutting into his territory."

"Whaddya mean?" the second girl asked again. "We didn't do anything."

"Just by agreeing to do something is soliciting. And, unless you want to be sex trafficked, get out of here now," I warned.

"Who do you think you are?" asked the first girl. "We have rights, ya know."

"Well, you won't have any rights if you stick around here. Now get the fuck out of here before I report you," I retorted as anger washed over me.

"Are you a cop?" asked the third girl, scared.

"Worse. Now git!" They hurriedly left bills on the table and scrambled out of there.

I went back to my table and waited to see who else would come in. Just before I rose to leave, a girl I recognized who'd been hanging out with Lulu when I was there last stepped into the bar. I caught her eye and waved her over. I slipped a $20 bill on the table and asked if she'd sit down for just a minute. I pushed the clipping toward her. "Do you recognize this girl?"

She covered the bill with her hand and slid it toward her, and popped it into her purse without breaking eye contact. She studied the clipping. "I think I might have. Blackie pulled in a lot of new girls before he was arrested. She might be one of them, but I can't be sure."

"Who's taking over for Blackie?"

"His partner, Stretch."

"Damn."

"He's taken over all of old downtown now."

"Wow, that's bad news. Those guys can be beasts."

"I know who you are—you're the lady counselor who helps girls. Things won't be good for you if you're caught here at this casino. I suggest you leave right now." She rose and headed back to the bar. Before she took too many steps, she called over her shoulder, "Stay safe, hear?"

CHAPTER 44

When I got back home, I thought of calling Sam but decided against it. It was too late. I readied myself for bed and turned in for the night.

Nightmares tore at me all night. I relived the last time I'd spoken to my parents.

"Tiffany, we want you to come home," stated her mother.

"I'm *not* coming home. Fuck that! Why would I," she scolded, "when everything I could ever want is right here?"

"We called your office to speak to you. They said you no longer work there and haven't for several months now... "

"How dare you check up on me!" she shouted.

"We just want what's best for you," defended her mother.

"And how would you even begin to know what's best for me? All you ever cared about was how pretty I was."

"That's not true, and you know it. You're the one who insisted on becoming a model."

"Well, you certainly took up the bragging rights for that, didn't you?"

"Robert?" her mother pleaded to her husband.

"Your mother and I think you should come home so you can get your life back in order."

"Well, you can forget that. I'm not living in a boring place with nothing to do—and you can't make me."

"Tiffany, let's not argue," pleaded her mother. "We simply want to help you …"

"That's such bullshit! If you want to help me, why don't you lay off me? You always want me to do things your way."

"Listen, Tiffany, you sound upset. Why don't we call you back in a little while?" her mother urged.

"Better yet, why don't you never call me again …."

"Whoa, Tiffany," interrupted her father. "You don't mean that. So let's…

"Yes, I do mean that, Dad. When I'm ready to forgive you, I'll call you."

"Forgive us for what?" asked her mother in disbelief.

"You'll have to figure that out …" her words slurred before she let her phone slip through her fingers and passed out.

I woke up disoriented, tears streaming down my cheeks. Recalling the confrontation I'd had with my parents, as well as my reoccurring nightmare of babies dying, had me feeling sad and overwhelmed. I was so unhappy with what'd taken place in the past. What could I do about it now?

In my dream, there appeared an angel with a golden light surrounding her and a smile on her face. "Be kind to yourself," she said and kissed me on the forehead. "The past is the past. Begin anew." As I replayed the words in my mind, they sparked a hope in me that maybe I still had time to right some of the past.

As I lay there in my bed, I remembered one of my first college teachers telling me a story about herself. Before she could exonerate herself for what she'd done in the past, she'd needed to write down on paper what she believed her discretions had been. And she needed to look at them as if those words belonged to a client – one separate from herself. That'd helped her be objective and let go of what couldn't be changed. It allowed her to look toward the future without being tethered to her past. If that worked for her, then that was something I could do—and needed to do.

And what about the missing girl—the young girl my aunt was worried about? If I wanted to locate her, I needed to do more than talk to some of the girls on the street. I'd call Sam to see if he knew anything about Ellen.

As soon as he answered my call, his warmth flooded me. "Hey, Tiffany! What a surprise."

"Do you have time to see me today?"

"Are you asking me on a date?" he asked, laughter in his voice.

"Well… not exactly. I wanted to know if you would help me find a missing girl."

He was silent for a moment, and I quickly added, "If you meet with me, I'll bring that special coffee you like so much."

He cleared his throat. "I'm not so sure it's wise for you to get mixed up with any of the missing girls after what you've been through."

"Sometimes, we have no choice, Sam."

He sighed. "Okay, come on in, but don't add sugar to my coffee. I'm on a diet."

"You? That's crazy! You're fine the way you are." My face heated when I realized how that sounded.

"That's nice to know," he bantered.

"I'll be there in an hour, okay?" I asked, getting to the chase.

"Okay. See you then."

I got up to shower and dress, feeling excited about pursuing the missing girl. It made me feel as if I'd be doing something tangible if I found her—unlike counseling, which didn't always bring about results. I'd be thrilled to locate her and help her out of the rabbit hole she was in if she was part of Blackie's harem.

I walked into Sam's office with two fresh specialty coffees—one without sugar. I sat down and drew the newspaper clipping from my bag and handed it to him. "I received this from my aunt, who asked me if I'd look into this. The girl in the picture is the daughter of her next-door neighbor."

After reading it over, he said, "Let me check and see if someone has already reported her missing. I'll be right back."

A few minutes later, Sam returned with a huge binder filled with pictures and newspaper clippings. "Here, you can look through this."

"I thought that you computerized everything."

"We do. Sometimes we receive photos and clippings and keep them in binders like this by date. It sorta works like a backup system."

"Cool." I opened the binder and began my search.

A short time later, I'd found nothing. At the same time, Sam turned to me from his computer and said, "I don't see that Ellen has been reported missing. We'll have to add her to our list." Sam shook his head. "Amazingly, so many people, who've been reported missing here in Las Vegas, are in clear sight; we just can't easily identify them."

"What do you mean?"

"Many of the girls change their names and looks when they come here, wanting a new identity. When we ask about a missing girl, no one recognizes her or her birth name, and we lose out."

"That's too bad. What happens after we report Ellen missing?"

"We announce it at our morning meeting and pass out the photo for all to carry with them. The problem is that there are so many girls to search out."

"Sad, isn't it?"

"More than that, I think. It's become an epidemic in my mind. What do the girls coming here think is going to happen? They have no idea, and if we try to warn them and tell them to leave here and go back home, they don't want to hear it. They won't take our advice, and then it's too late."

"Maybe if we work together, we can find some of them …"

"Hold on there! That's not going to happen …"

"Why not?"

"You have no authority to get involved, and besides, right now, I don't think it's safe for you to get involved."

I hated it when someone tried to prevent me from doing what I wanted. "You do realize, don't you, that you have no legal right to stop me searching for anyone. Right, Sam?"

He paused and stared at me, saying nothing. "I said I'd help you with this one if I could. But that's it, understood? After that, you've got to stay out of it."

"But …!"

"Promise?"

I wasn't going to lie to Sam, so I remained silent. If he took that to mean I agreed, that was his problem. My new client was due soon, so I quickly said goodbye to Sam and left.

CHAPTER 45

After I left Sam, my heart felt lighter. With his help, maybe I could pull this off and get Ellen back to her parents, and that might open the door to healing the rift between my parents and me. For the first time, I believed it could happen.

For the rest of that day and the following two, I kept busy with my clients and even wrote an article for the upcoming magazine put out by the organization of counselors where I was a member. I'd been asked to write about our addiction to iPhones. That jolted me to realize that Ellen must have a cell phone. If she were part of Blackie's harem, it probably had been taken away from her. But still... it wouldn't hurt to find out if she had one.

I called Sam to ask if he'd contacted Ellen's parents, and if so, did he have Ellen's cell phone number?

"Another officer is looking into it." He sighed. "Just let us do our work. You promised, remember?"

"It's important to me to find this girl, Sam."

"I know. We're doing our best."

"Will you promise me that when you find her, you'll let me be the first to know? I want to be there to help her adjust after what she's been through."

"I'll see what I can do."

"Please. I'd really appreciate it."

"Tiffany, I've got to go. I'll call you later, okay?"

"Okay," I answered.

Unwilling to leave everything in the hands of the police, I thought of a way I could flush Ellen out. I knew the name of the call center that Blackie still used to peddle his prostitutes, and it'd be easy enough to look up the telephone number. I'd call there and pretend to be someone interested in paying for a toss in the hay with a young girl who was rather virginal and inexperienced. I'd ask to have photos of the girls texted to me so I could decide among them. I might get lucky. And trying this was better than doing nothing.

I did my research and found the telephone number I wanted. I cleared my throat several times and practiced speaking in a lower tone. At last, I picked up my prepaid cell phone and punched in the numbers. It was answered right away by a woman with a sweet voice.

"This is Virginia speaking. How may we pleasure you?"

I rolled my eyes at her greeting and told her what I wanted. She suggested that I go onto their website to make the arrangements. "We use codes for identifying some of your choices, and you'll be able to see pictures of the girls available for what you want. You can call back here if you have any questions."

Immediately, I understood her tactic. It was a way to cut out the "shaft from the wheat," and to represent their setup as more of a legitimate business. I was pretty sure I'd be able to understand their codes just from having been on the streets. I thanked her and hung up the phone, anxious to see what I could discover. I wanted to bring in the other angels on my mission to find Ellen. I'd drive out to the ranch after my last client to go over things with them, and then I'd stay there for the weekend.

Driving out to the ranch, I was excited to become proactive in searching for Ellen. I had a feeling this would be right up Linda's alley too because she'd complained lately that her search on the internet for plots in human trafficking had broadened with the availability of the worldwide web. The reality was that human trafficking had only increased. The sad part was that the United States was second in the world for the number of porno sites that displayed real-time abuse of children. Many of those same perpetrators were trying to figure out ways to hide their location on the internet since what they were doing on the internet, email, and social media sites had become a threat to them. Most often, what they did could be traced back to them.

When I turned into the ranch, I was surprised to see that Lucy and Lester's car was there. That was unusual, and I wondered what'd happened to bring them out to our neck of the woods. It was unusually quiet as I approached the house, and I didn't hear a sound as I opened the front door. "Anybody here?" I called out.

A somber Betsy came forward from the kitchen and waved to me to follow her. Lucy and Lester were sitting at the kitchen table, along with the other angels. All looked downcast and gloomy. "What's happened?" I asked as I took my seat.

Something terrible, I thought, upon seeing Jerome and Sarah outside while the rest of us were sitting inside. It was apparent they'd ask Jerome to keep Sarah out of the way.

"Here, read this," said Lucy pushing a piece of paper toward me.

I took the note from her, and after reading it, I looked up and said, "She's dead?"

They nodded. "I don't believe it," I said. "After this last round of struggling to get clean and sober, I thought she had a chance for success. Poor Sue-Ling."

I reread the note. "I'm done. I can't fight it anymore. I'll never be free of the drugs. Life sucks. Sue-Ling." It'd been addressed to Lucy and Lester.

I felt especially sorry for Lester and Lucy since it was the first of the girls we'd helped who hadn't made it through. The rest of us angels had seen this kind of thing before, and as painful as it was, her death wasn't entirely unexpected.

"How did it happen?" I asked.

"Sue-Ling asked the nurse for a sleeping pill to help her sleep. So later, when the nurse's shift ended, she told the oncoming nurse that Sue-Ling had finally gotten to sleep and to let her sleep. They didn't know she'd stolen some pills, had saved them up and swallowed them. So later, when the second nurse checked on her, she thought she was still asleep. The next time the nurse checked on her, it was too late."

"Are there going to be any charges against the nurse or hospital?" I asked.

"No," said Lester.

"I feel so sorry for Sue-Ling's mother. Now this, after losing her brother," said Missy.

"We're going to take care of what she wants done with Sue-Ling's body," said Lester. "And the uncle's too if needed."

Lucy pushed herself up from her chair. "We'd better get going, Lester," she said in a tired voice.

"Aren't you joining us for dinner?" asked Missy.

"Right now, I don't think I could swallow a thing and keep it down," Lucy said. "Besides, we've got a lot to do with the arrangements and all."

The rest of us got up from the kitchen table and walked Lucy and Lester to the front door, where we hugged and kissed our goodbyes. Sarah came running out onto the porch with a scowl. "Papa, you weren't going to leave without saying goodbye to me, were you?"

"Of course not. You'd never let us get away with that, would you, little one?"

"Not on your life," she announced.

We all laughed. "Where did you come up with that expression, Sarah?" asked Betsy.

"Jerome said that when I asked him if he wanted to ride Big Red."

We laughed again, and the somber mood temporarily lightened a bit. We stood together on the porch and watched Lucy and Lester drive away. At last, we turned away and walked back inside, our hearts heavy with remorse over Sue-Ling's death.

Now was not the time to discuss Ellen with the others. It'd have to wait. Tomorrow was another day, and that'd be soon enough.

CHAPTER 46

The next morning I awoke with a clearer idea about how we could track down Ellen. The smell of muffins fresh from the oven called to me, and I hurriedly made my way downstairs with Scout at my heels. It was a lazy Saturday morning, and I hoped that Linda and Jerome hadn't made plans to go off for the day as they'd recently been doing.

I was surprised that I was the last one to the table. Usually, Linda and Jerome were the last to join us. "Good morning, everyone!" I said in a cheery voice as I opened the door for Scout to go out and went to pour myself a cup of freshly brewed coffee.

I drew everyone's attention. "You certainly sound glad to be alive this morning," said Missy.

"And so I am," I said, returning her smile. "I have something I want to discuss with all of you."

"Okay. Is it something private?" asked Betsy, tipping her head toward Sarah.

I knew she was asking if what I had to say was okay for Sarah to hear. "Sarah, what we're going to discuss is pretty boring. Why don't you pick out a puzzle that you and I can do later?"

"Okay, Auntie Tiff. But I want to watch my show first. Can I, Mommy?"

"Yes, you can. After that, though, the television goes off, understand?"

"Yeess." We smiled as Sarah dramatically flounced out of the room.

Expectant eyes turned to me. "I received an interesting piece of mail a few days ago." I passed around the card and the newspaper clipping. I filled them in on my conversation with Sam, and then I told them how by using Linda and Jerome's expertise, I thought we could seek her out.

"Not only do we have Blackie's website given to me by his office receptionist, but there are other websites that specialize in girl prostitutes from Las Vegas. You two know ways to work it, so if you request one of the girls, it can't be traced back to you, right?"

"We hide our tracks all the time," Jerome said.

"Another thing we can do is go onto our local website that lists missing girls to see if there is a match between them and the girls on these prostitution sites. By pretending we're interested in hiring the girls, maybe we'll be able to find out if they'd been sex trafficked or not and want out. We could help them that way."

"Although that sounds easy enough to do, it's not," said Linda. "There are other considerations, such as the safeguards in place for the pimps to protect their employees. Remember, sometimes a guard will go with the girls on a job, especially if the girl is new and didn't choose to do this on their own. I've seen some girls on the sites wearing bracelets with homing devices on their ankles. Disgustingly enough, that can be a turn-on for some of the johns."

"So, there's nothing we can do?" I asked.

"Oh, I'm not saying that at all," Linda said. "It's just that we have to be very careful about how we approach Blackie's site as a john."

"Why not discover where Blackie's partner is keeping the girl and then rescue her from there?" asked Betsy.

"That's a good idea, especially since Sam and the police are doing their own thing to find Ellen. We could work together with Linda and Jerome searching out the hiding place for the newbie girls and the police raiding it after we let them know it's location."

"That sounds like a lot safer way to handle this," said Missy. "We don't want anything to happen to the girls."

We nodded and murmured our agreements. I gave the clipping to Jerome and told him the name of Blackie's website. "Well then, shall we get started, boo?" he asked as he grabbed Linda's hand and pulled her up from her chair.

Missy said she wanted to collect more eggs from the henhouse, and she left Betsy and me sitting at the table with our newly-filled coffee mugs. "I read on the card that your aunt said your parents send their love. Were you surprised to see that?" Betsy asked.

I nodded. "Yes, I was. You know, Betsy, it probably sounds odd, but I think if I can locate Ellen and return her safely home to her parents as my aunt asked me to do, I'd be making up for some of my past. Weird, huh?"

"Not really. Ever since you've become involved with Sam, things have been different with you. You've brought up your past several times, hinting at the possibility that maybe it was time to change things between you and your parents." Betsy chuckled. "Or maybe it's because we insisted that you can't have a healthy relationship with a man until you've forgiven yourself for the past mistakes that have gotten you to think differently."

"Perhaps," I responded as my face reddened, which made Betsy's smile broaden.

"Listen, sister. It's time to love yourself despite yourself. We girls have told you that before. There's your power, girlfriend—no doubt about it. Love yourself, and the world is yours," Betsy said. "Forgiveness is your freedom."

I knew she was right. I filled with love for her and the other angels, and most of all, for Lucy and Lester. I was so grateful for my connection to them, and now I knew it was time to consider including the blessings of my parents. And I had a feeling that perhaps it would include Sam too, down the road. There was much to think about, that was for sure.

The weekend closed with no additional information regarding Ellen's whereabouts, and I ended up driving back to town Sunday night feeling uplifted despite having no progress regarding Ellen. I'd made up my mind to write to my parents the next morning to begin healing the break between us. And, please God, hoped that they'd be open to it.

CHAPTER 47

The next morning, true to my promise to myself, I took paper and pen to write an apology to my parents and to tell them I was sorry for hurting them.

"Dear Mom and Dad,

I don't know if you'll ever be able to forgive me, but…"

Once I started to write, I couldn't stop. I wrote page after page of what'd happened to me, the saving grace of Lucy and Lester, and all the other Angels, including Sarah. I wrote about everything except my abortion. I'd learned that each of us is allowed some privacy—a separate pain or separate pleasure not to be shared. I signed my letter, "Your loving daughter," and nearly crossed it out, believing I hadn't earned that right.

Then I decided to hell with it—in for a penny, in for a pound.

I was exhausted after I'd completed my letter, which seemed more like a novella by the time I'd finished. I stuffed it into an 8"x11" envelope and waited for the mailman to come so I could give it to him.

Not much later, I heard the mailman at the front door, and without hesitating, I grabbed the envelope to hand him. When I suddenly opened the door, I surprised him, and we laughed together at the silliness of it all. When I held out the envelope for him to take, I had second thoughts. Was I ready to proceed? Still debating with myself, I was startled when he snatched it from my hand, placed it into his mailbag, and turned to leave. Too late to change my mind now, I thought with a flighty feeling in my stomach. I'd have to wait and see what would happen.

Several days passed when I received a phone call from Linda telling me that she and Jerome were pretty sure they'd found Blackie's hiding place for his trafficked girls. "I'll send you the address so that you can deal with Sam yourself."

I called Sam, and he wasn't there, so I left a message for him to please call me after he returned. I was antsy and became distracted during my session with my last client of the day. I ended up not charging her for our time together and asked her to return the following week for another session.

I jumped when the phone rang, and my stomach did a somersault when I saw it was Sam. "Hi Sam, its Tiffany," I said automatically.

He laughed. "I know who you are since I'm the one who called you. What's happening?"

"I know where Blackie and his partner are hiding his new girls. I'll bet that Ellen is among them. I want to be there when you and the other police bust in."

"Whoa! First of all, how do you know Blackie's location?"

When I didn't answer, he interjected, "Your friends, right?"

"Yes," I answered.

"I definitely want to meet these friends of yours."

"One day soon, I promise."

"What's the address?"

"Promise me that I can be there too?"

"I think I can arrange that if you remain outside and not interfere."

"I will, I promise. I want to be there so I can explain to Ellen why you're there and how I got involved. I think that'll help to ease her mind."

"The address?"

After I gave it to him, he asked, "Are you sure? I just looked it up, and there's nothing there but an abandoned building that used to be a veterinarian's office."

"Yes, that's the address given to me, so I'm sure."

"Okay. I'll get back to you. I have to take this to my boss and get approval for the raid, which won't be tonight. We have to do our own surveillance before we can move on it."

"Why? I've told you where he keeps the girls. Isn't that enough?"

"Think about it, Tiffany. It's not that I don't believe you, but we have to make sure that we have reason to move on it. We can't take a chance to raid the place only to find we've been on a wild goose chase because someone gave us a tip without us doing our part."

"I guess ..."

"Listen, I'll get back to you. I promise."

"Okay. I'm going to hold you to it."

"I can think of nothing better than holding you," he quipped.

I groaned. "You're such a guy," I said in mock disapproval.

"I'm glad you noticed," he teased.

I laughed, a warm feeling spreading across my body. "I'll talk to you later, Sam."

After we hung up, I scolded myself. "You have a lot to learn about how things happen on the other side of the law, Tiffany." Sam was one of the good guys, and I felt with him on my side, we could get Ellen out of her mess and save her from a lot of grief. I sure hoped that was so.

CHAPTER 48

When I hadn't heard anything from Sam by the next afternoon, I called him. He answered on the first ring. "Hi there, Tiffany," he whispered, obviously in a meeting. "We're getting approval to raid the place tonight. Can you make it to the police station by six o'clock? You can ride with Shirley and me."

"Okay. But ..."

"Oops. Gotta go."

My heart began to pound with excitement. I'd be so happy to find Ellen and whoever else needed help. I'd applied for and had received my permit to carry a gun, but I didn't know if I should take it with me. I'd decide later.

I called Linda and told her what was going on and to share the information with the other angels. "You're not going inside there with the police, are you? You'll be outside where it's safe, right?" she asked.

"Of course. That's the agreement I made with Sam."

"Well, good luck then. Let us know right away, okay?"

"Yup. Will do."

After saying goodbye to Linda, I sensed that I should take my gun with me. So I went to where I stored it and dropped it into my giant purse. The doorbell rang, and I went to let in my last client for the day.

Just before 5:30 p.m., I loaded into my car and headed to the police station. When I arrived there, I saw more than the usual number of vehicles parked in the lot, and there was noticeable excitement in the air. At one point, I saw Sam in the distance and waved my hand to let him know I had arrived. I stayed outside in the parking lot and stood beside Sam's car to wait for him and Shirley while several cops flitted around.

When Sam came closer, his smile seemed forced as he held out a bulletproof vest. "Here, put this on. I don't want anything to happen to you."

"Okay, but you have nothing to worry about. I'll be right here in the car, and I'm not going anywhere."

His eyes softened, and he smiled with tenderness. "Good."

"Ready, you two?" asked Shirley as she came up to us. She opened the back door and said, "You're back here, Tiffany."

It was interesting to sit behind Sam and Shirley and watch the interplay between them. Shirley was older than Sam and more experienced, which she liked to remind him of it in a kidding way. It was evident that they were fond of each other, and they seemed to work well together. I felt safe and protected with them in control.

The FBI was part of this bust, and Sam and Shirley weren't too happy about the man in charge, but they were following his lead because that was part of their job. I sensed that if the man heading this knew I was along for the ride, he'd be unhappy about it and block me from remaining there. Since I didn't want that to happen, I'd have to make sure I kept well-hidden. As we pulled in with the other vehicles, I sloughed down in my seat so my head wouldn't show.

"Stay down and keep safe," Sam whispered as he opened his door and got out to join the others.

While dusk was settling in, we'd parked a safe distance away from the vet's building, the last car to pull in. It would soon be dark, making the FBI agents dressed in black hard to see. I rose from my seat and peeked out and saw several cops on the roof of the building next door to the vet's dilapidated building. I could make out others creeping close to the building with their guns drawn. It looked just like it did in the movies, only this time there was no handsome actor to ensure there'd be no actual deaths. It was the real deal, and my heart pounded.

There was a deadly silence as I watched the cops and FBI agents move forward without creating a sound. I saw two of them crack open a side door and go inside with others following behind. The rest surrounded the building leaving no escape for anyone wanting out. I waited with bated breath.

All was quiet until it wasn't. Everything seemed to happen at once. I heard gunshots and people screaming—both men and girls. Then a short while later, a man came to the doorway, holding a gun against the head of a young girl and ordered everyone to drop their weapons and move out of the way. He looked around, searching for an escape. A thought flashed before me. I knew with certainty that he was going to try to escape in the car I was in, the only one not closed in by other vehicles. I prepared myself to deal with it as he dragged the girl along with him and came my way. I pulled my gun from my bag and released the safety. I thought of Sam and what he'd said about the power of a gun and the difference between using it to kill or to protect. Since I still held such anger against men who used women for their own sexual needs without consideration of the other person, I was conflicted. I was afraid that my emotions would make my actions a knee-jerk reaction.

Time seemed to slow down with each step the man took toward me, and only at the last second after hearing the girl cry out did I react. I raised my gun, and when the door opened, and the light came on, I was able to get a clear shot as he pushed the girl away from him and began to lower himself into the driver's seat. I held my hands steady as I'd been taught to do and yelled, "Got ya now, you bastard." He startled, and I pulled the trigger.

It was the perpetrator's high-pitched screaming that had thumping feet running toward us. Sam was the first to reach me. His relief at my safety was evident before he grabbed me and held me tight in his arms as if never to let me go. I realized then that I had fallen in love with him enough to want to make room for him in my life. Shirley came up to us, and when she saw me, she exclaimed. "Thank God!" Then, she nudged Sam. "What's the matter with you? Kiss her," she ordered as she bent to the hysterical young girl sitting on the ground.

And he did—thoroughly.

As more people came close, Sam and I separated. I went to the young girl, who Shirley was holding in her arms, to see if she was Ellen. She wasn't. I could see that although the girl had been drugged, she appeared coherent enough to understand my question, "Are there more girls inside?"

The girl nodded, and through her tears, she grabbed my arm and pleaded. "Don't leave me."

Those words had been the same ones that I'd spoken to Lester many years before. Yes, I'd keep my promise to this girl and the others as Lucy and Lester had done for me. I'd make sure they got the help they needed to feel loved and safe once more.

"You're safe with Shirley; stay here," I told the girl as I left her to run inside to see if Ellen was with the other girls. I pushed my way inside the building and was barely able to keep from throwing up when I saw about a dozen girls who had been locked into the cages where the vet had kept dogs. Trying not to be noticed, each girl huddled in the farthest corner of their cage. Several ambulances had been called, and some of the medics were already checking out the girls found there. I walked up and down the two aisles of cages searching for Ellen. In the last cage, hunched in the corner, a young girl sat, hiding underneath a blanket she'd thrown over herself. "Ellen?" I called. "Is that you, Ellen?"

The girl shuffled and moved around. I stepped forward. "Ellen? Your mother sent me to look for you. They love you and miss you. Can you remove your blanket, please?"

After a bit, she lowered the blanket, and I wanted to cry when I saw the fear and sadness in her pretty face. She wasn't the first, and I knew she wouldn't be the last of the girls we'd help out of their rabbit holes. It seemed like such an uphill battle to stop the human trafficking and abuse of minors and women. Yes, and boys too. But Lucy was right when she said it had to begin with removing the pimps who sold their "employees" to the johns. As well, it had to be a concerted effort on everyone's part to destroy the sites that offered porn and the observance of exploited children sexually abused in real-time. We had to kill it on the internet just like Linda was trying to do.

I reached for Ellen and enclosed her in my arms. She felt frail, and I practically had to carry her along with me as we headed out to the nearest ambulance. I forced my way into the ambulance with Ellen, and we drove to the nearest hospital. Shirley was in another ambulance with the girl who'd asked us not to leave her alone. I'd made my promise to her, and with Lester and Lucy's help, I'd keep it.

CHAPTER 49

That night was the beginning of several weeks of stress, anxiety, and several miracles.

I was called into the station to answer to the head of the FBI. He was none too pleased with Sam for allowing me to be on-site at the time of their raid. However, he reluctantly agreed that it was a good idea to have a counselor or a person from a non-profit dealing with human trafficking on hand to help soothe the girls during their abrupt transition. He told me he hadn't worked out yet how he was going to define my role in the raid and asked me not to say anything about it. I promised I wouldn't because I didn't want the notoriety of being a gunslinger. Sam had laughed at that.

My parents wrote me a long letter telling me how much they loved me and wanted to see me. They made it very clear that the past was the past, and they were only interested in a new beginning.

Ellen and I had several sessions together, where she was able to talk about what'd happened to her. She'd faked the pills given to her to keep her drugged, and was realistic about how her choices had gotten her to where she was now. She was remarkable in her recovery. Her parents were loving and encouraging, allowing her to stay in Las Vegas to heal before flying her home. I'd be going with her, at which time I'd have the opportunity to visit my parents.

Sam and I grew closer. Although it seemed obvious to everyone else who knew Sam, I was beginning to understand that he'd been in love with me for years—ever since he'd turned me down that time I'd propositioned him. At this point in our relationship, I knew that I couldn't keep putting Sam off regarding his wanting to meet my friends. So I asked Lester, Lucy, and the angels to meet with me to see how they felt about exposing Sam to them.

"So, what are you asking us?" Lester asked. "Do you want to bring Sam here to the ranch for dinner?"

We girls smiled at Lester's question. As a man, he didn't understand that my bringing Sam to the ranch meant more than a meal.

"Lester, I think you've missed Tiffany's point," said Lucy, gently patting his hand.

"I think the point should be, do you love Sam? Missy gently asked.

"More to the point," said Linda. "Have you forgiven your past choices and feel free now to move ahead?"

"Even more to the point," said Betsy, "have you learned to love yourself, and are you ready to face life without dragging the past with you?"

I began to laugh with great joy—for all my beautiful angels and what they represented. Without understanding my reason for laughing, one by one, they all joined in, and we laughed together.

After catching our breath, Lester announced, "For heaven sakes, Tiff, of course, you can invite Sam here for dinner."

With that comment, we began to roar with laughter again—enough so that it caused Jerome and Sarah to join in.

Later that night, before Lester and Lucy left, Lucy slipped upstairs to speak to me. She pushed Scout over to make room for herself and sat down on my bed. "I want to tell you how proud I am of you. You've come a long way from the first time I saw you. The best thing you've done is that you are learning to love—love all that is, all that was. People think to love someone or something, you have to like it and agree with it. That isn't true. As a mother and your soul sister, I give you this piece of advice. Show Sam off to all those you care about and show him the love he deserves simply for loving you, and you'll have a happy life. I promise you that."

Lucy leaned forward and kissed me. I grabbed her and pulled her closer. "I love you, my dear friend. How can I ever repay you?"

"Why what a silly question," Lucy said as she rose and walked to the door, turning at the last minute. "Just be happy."

I sat in bed, staring after Lucy, thinking about what she'd said. A few minutes later, my cell phone rang. When I saw it was my parents, my heart lifted. I listened to what they had to say and smiled as I answered their question.

"Yes, I'd love to visit, Mom and Dad! And I'll be bringing someone with me. I want you to meet Sam."

Wait, there's more...

I remember as a young girl occasionally overhearing words that I found disturbing without knowing its meaning: prostitution, rape, and incest were some of them. Perhaps it was the way it was whispered, out of earshot, and beyond my knowledge or comprehension. No matter what, those words brought about bad feelings that stuck with me. It was only when I got older and learned their meaning that I understood their mixed message of abuse played out as love. And the heartache of it was that kind of behavior was and is so far-reaching.

As an author, I'm aware that the written word has a power of its own to influence others. I can use my writing to express concerns or draw attention to the ways of living that hurt and disempower others. For those of you who have read my mystery Death Card series of books, you will see that idea as part of my storyline.

In Angels Out of the Dark, I have once again chosen to bring the awareness of human trafficking into the storyline with a lighter touch. I also present the possibility of recovery when you have the right people surrounding you. My goal was to write this book (and the others) in such a way to provide you, the reader, with an incentive to step forward and do what you can to disallow human trafficking.

Las Vegas has four or five people a day who go missing! What happens to them? Where do they go? Las Vegas is one of the principal cities in the west caught in the corridor of sex trafficking, prostitution, and drugs. What can we do about it?

Fortunately, right here in Las Vegas, we have hardworking non-profits that deal with all aspects of human trafficking. One of those groups is interested in bringing *awareness* to the public regarding human trafficking. I wanted to meet the woman who headed that non-profit, and a mutual friend introduced us via email. I was excited and intrigued to meet Lena Walther, the honorary consul from Sweden, who also is a co-founder of the non-profit AIP (Awareness is Prevention).

I was not disappointed. Lena is an attractive, pleasant, bright, and energetic woman who is determined to do all she can to alleviate the ever-growing threat of human trafficking. It is because of people like her doing what they can to make more people aware of what's going on in our shadows of living that children, women, and men can be safe from the pitfalls of human trafficking.

After discussing with Lena about what I could do to help her and her agency, I realized that the best way for me to bring awareness of human trafficking to others was by writing Angels Out of the Dark in the same fashion as I had the Death Card Series. However, I didn't want to step away from providing the reader with the real skinny on human trafficking and how it works. So, I asked Lena if she would be so kind as to write an article about what she'd learned, and I'd use it as an addendum to the book. She happily agreed.

Here is what Lena had to say:

What is Human Trafficking, also referred to as Modern Day Slavery? How does it differ from Prostitution? These are questions many people ask. The definition of prostitution is "the business or activity of engaging in sexual activity in exchange for payment." That is, paid for sexual services, if you will. Sex trafficked victims, on the other hand, do not benefit from the sexual activity, typically, as all of their earnings are taken and controlled by their pimp, or handler, or trafficker. Also, prostitution is generally between consenting adults of legal age. Victims of sex trafficking are as young as ten years old for girls and around nine years old for boys. Because kids of this age are not capable of making rational decisions about sexual encounters, it is automatically a felony to engage in sex with minors 17 years old and under, and the victims are not arrested or booked as prostitutes. Newer laws have come into existence the past few years that can delete the criminal records of young people caught up in the sex trafficking industry.

Prostitution is the oldest profession in the world. Sex trafficking, on the other hand, is the new form of Slavery and is much worse since it focuses so much on children because they are easier to manipulate and control. Since they are treated as chattel, to be sold over and over again, the younger they are, the longer they can be traded. Labor trafficking is prevalent in more underdeveloped countries where they promise good jobs and new lives when one signs on to work. However, to repay for their transportation, food, and protection, the victim seldom earns enough money to pay off their "contract." They have no identification and are threatened with being turned over to the police or, more bluntly, death. The labor traffickers also have no qualms about ending the life of a person who is no longer a productive worker. The victims have no identification and no communication with the outside world. They are living from day to day, performing grueling labor on a boat, an agricultural site, or another place that has an unregulated labor force. On a boat, the victim may become chum for fishing. In a field, some have never returned from the area they were working in. There have been several instances of having young women service the field workers as part of their obligations to their traffickers. It is an insidious world.

The misconception that trafficking only happens to "those foreign girls and boys" and that it does not exist in our Western Culture could not be further from the truth. What most people don't realize is that anyone can fall victim to being trafficked... anyone. Sex Trafficking is more common in our part of the world and also the fastest-growing "business" worldwide. And, coincidentally, the most profitable one. It has surpassed Arms and Drug Trafficking in terms of profitability. To the trafficker, it is strictly about money. Most of the proceeds are all cash and almost impossible to trace.

The patterns used to persuade a potential victim may vary, but the ultimate goal is the same. The goal is to gain complete control over a person and instill enough fear, so they don't dare to try to leave or work against their trafficker. Often the victims are beset with what is called the "Stockholm Syndrome." It is where they identify with, and even protect their captor because of their dependence on him for survival. They are brainwashed and have been cultured to safeguard their "Owner" as a first reaction. It takes a lot of bravery to turn against him/her as they have lost their sense of worth and independence.

Again, the younger the victims, the easier they are to control. Often a young victim is recruited via social media or other non-face-to-face encounters.

Sometimes, they are even challenged to be accepted by a trafficker, pretending to be a person of the same age, to send compromising photos over their cell phones.

Porn is another tool the traffickers use to groom and instill what is required of the victim. Younger and younger kids are viewing porn as it is readily available on their mobile phones. What they see to them is the norm, and the boundaries are unfathomable. Child pornography is increasing, and some sectors of the population advocate for its legalization as just another sexual preference. But when one listens to the outpouring of the rescued or liberated children, one realizes that their childhood has been robbed from them, and their trauma will be with them forever. Doctors revealing so much about their patients' trauma has created considerable opposition to lowering the penalties or lowering the age of consent.

Of course, becoming a victim in the sex industry happens to adults as well. There is no rhyme or reason on whom they prey. Some traffickers may rely on an older victim to be his partner in recruiting, establishing rules, and even disciplining the younger victims. They can be vicious. It has been documented that the older participants, primarily women, may have started as young victims themselves. However, the survivability of a trafficked victim is usually relatively short-lived. They either become susceptible to overuse of drugs, sicknesses, and STDs or just physical abuse, which shortens their lives.

There are so many stories by survivors that are both heart-rending and tragic. That is why we must spread awareness of the traps of becoming a victim and how to avoid it. It is much more effective to prevent a bad situation, through knowledge, training, and education, than trying to rescue, rehabilitate, and save the life of a victim.

That is primarily the reason why Awareness is Prevention (AIP) was formed. Additionally, AIP is at the forefront in helping change the legislation to enact other laws that would punish the purveyors and solicitors of child sex trafficking. Working at the higher levels of both International, Federal, and State levels is a prime objective.

The most vulnerable children are the typically shy and needy kids we see every day. Whether it is in their apparent lack of self-esteem or the lack of life's essentials, such as the homeless youth, a trafficker will pick up on that condition and try to exploit it. Children are always craving to be cared for and loved. They may not have a family that provides the environment for being loved or nurtured. Also, they will succumb to the excitement of trying new things when presented to them by a trafficker who is trying to recruit them. Their naïve curiosity, and the temptations offered by the traffickers, are hard to resist, especially in the cultural climate we see today.

The sexualizing of practically every aspect of our lives normalizes youthful sex and lifestyles that are not healthy. The fast-paced environment depicted on

TV, the music, and the provocative advertisements all play into the fast life idolized today. The kids are the perfect prey. The traffickers in the "Grooming" phase will lavish the potential victim with gifts, make-up, excellent food, and even drugs to win them over. The goal is to make them fall in love with their "Romeo." As part of their grooming phase, the victim may be asked to participate in a "photoshoot" or video production or a private sex tape. Once a visual record is made, it can be turned on them as blackmail by threatening to reveal it to the parents or put on the Internet for all their friends and relatives to view. Sometimes, that is used in conjunction with threatening the new victim that the traffickers will harm their immediate family if they refuse to cooperate with the escalation of more demanding sexual tasks. Gangs are a significant factor in the trafficking trade these days.

We can never stop Trafficking completely. However, the best weapon to use to get a handle on it is through Education and Training. The more people that are aware, the better they can prevent becoming a victim and see the warning signs before it is too late.

AIP's mission is to Educate and Train as many people as possible, whether it is Law Enforcement, First Responders, Educators, Students, Parents, other NGOs, and the general public. The list goes on.

Traffickers are narcissists, often charismatic and quite often sociopaths. They charm not only their victims but also everyone else around them. Eventually, they will take full control. Victims are told not to tell anyone. If they do, their loved ones may be killed or punished. The chain binding the victim is not a physical one; it is an invisible, mental one. The fear is beyond what most of us can understand.

In summation, awareness is a viable solution to help stop the insidious crimes against our youth and others who are vulnerable. Awareness must be done right, must be widespread, and become an integral part of a child's fundamental knowledge base.

For more information or to support the non-profit in its need to stop human trafficking go to Awareness is Prevention at www.AIPNV.ORG.

Lena Walther
Co-Founder and Executive Director
Awareness Is Prevention (AIP)

J.S. PECK

Joan was reared in a family of readers in small-town Elmira, New York. Each Sunday afternoon was a special time where each member of her family was able to relax with a good book. She was raised to be opened-minded, and discussion about her beliefs was encouraged. Joan came to the understanding that we are all connected energetically and can communicate with others who have passed on. Drawn to her spiritual and supernatural beliefs, Joan brings that idea into all of her writings and expresses in her work her interest to shatter the power of addiction and human trafficking.

Joan is an editor and author of short stories, spiritual books, and has a mystery book series called The Death Card Series. Her book, Prime Threat – Shattering the Power of Addiction, has helped many who are looking to understand addiction in a whole new way. She is also a contributing writer for Choices magazine and serves as the Editor in Chief for Chic Compass magazine, produced in Las Vegas and available world-wide.

"I hope you enjoyed reading this book. If so, and you feel inspired, please help other readers discover it by leaving your honest review on Amazon.com., Goodreads, or Bookbub. Reviews are what helps an author to succeed. Thank you for your kindness."